THE MAN WHO WAS POE

Also by Avi

Escape from Home:
Beyond the Western Sea Book One

Into the Storm:
Beyond the Western Sea Book Two

Midnight Magic

Murder at Midnight

Nothing But the Truth

Perloo the Bold

Romeo and Juliet Together (and Alive!) at Last

Something Upstairs

The True Confessions of Charlotte Doyle

THE MAN WHO WAS POE

WHO WAS POE

AVI

SCHOLASTIC INC.

FOR DOROTHY MARKINKO

This book was originally published in hardcover by Orchard Books in 1989.

ISBN 978-0-545-50523-9

12 11 10 9 8 7 6 5 4 3 2 1   13 14 15 16 17 18/0

Printed in the U.S.A. 40
This edition first printing, July 2013

CONTENTS

PROVIDENCE, RHODE ISLAND

NOVEMBER 1848

PROLOGUE

AT THE FAR back of the top floor of an Ann Street tenement was a room. It was a small, single-windowed room, not much warmer than the outside, for there was only a solitary candle to heat it. The room contained a table, a chair, and against one wall, a trunk. Opposite the trunk was a narrow bed upon which sat a boy. His name was Edmund.

He was a frail boy, as thin as the clothes he wore, with light hair and a face both sad and pale. His knees were drawn up and he was hugging them, head down. But all the while he was watching his sister.

Sis — that was Edmund's name for her — was a little taller than her brother, her hair a shade lighter, but otherwise they shared a close resemblance. She was sitting by the table, a blanket draped across her shoulders. Her feet, in high-buttoned shoes, were hooked over the lower rung of the chair. Open before her lay a tattered book of fairy tales. But it had been hours since she'd read a word.

"Edmund?" she said in a low, empty voice.

"What?"

"How long is it now?"

"Two days."

Sis continued to stare at the door. Then, in a breaking voice, she said, "But what *reason* could there *be* for Aunty staying away so long?"

Edmund sighed. "She must have some."

"That's what you always say."

Edmund squirmed uncomfortably.

"Do you truly think it has to do with Mum?" Sis continued.

"I'm sure it does," Edmund said. "Aunty's found her and together they've taken a lovely house. They're only making it right for us."

"Do you believe that?"

"I want to," Edmund said.

Sis leaned over the table again and made another attempt to read. Edmund could see she was too weary.

"I'm beastly hungry," she said finally.

Edmund closed his eyes.

Sis took a coin out of her pocket and placed it on the table. "We've got a half dime left," she announced.

"I know."

"It could buy something."

4

Edmund shook his head. "Aunty said we were not to go out, that we were to stay here."

"But Edmund," Sis cried. "Something must have happened to her! In all the month we've been here, in all her going about and looking for Mum, never once has she kept away this long. Now has she?"

"No," Edmund admitted.

"And we've eaten everything we had. She wouldn't want us to starve, would she?"

"We promised not to go out," Edmund said resolutely. "What if we went and she returned? She might think something awful had happened to us. It would be a dreadful shock. You know the way she is."

"It's you who mind her so," Sis said. "I don't."

Edmund looked down. How many times had he explained to Sis that since he was the sole man of the family, he had a responsibility to meet. Going out at this hour would have been dangerous enough in England, their home, but here in America, where they were still strangers . . . No, the safest thing to do was to obey Aunty.

"We'd only be gone a tiny bit," Sis coaxed.

"No."

"Then you go," Sis said suddenly. "I'll stay."

Edmund lifted his head. "Alone?"

"Somebody has to!"

"Nothing will be open."

"That saloon on Wickenden keeps night hours. They might have something there."

5

"Aunty says it's a wicked place."

"Oh, Edmund," Sis cried, "Aunty Pru isn't here! We have to do for ourselves! And if you won't, I will."

For a long while Edmund said nothing. But when he saw a tear trickle down his sister's cheek he drew himself to his feet. From his pocket he took out a key. "I'll go on one condition," he said. "I'll lock the door once I'm out. That way no one but me can get in and I'll feel better about leaving you."

"Edmund, really!" she said as she pressed the half dime into his hand. "Nothing will happen. You'll be only a few moments."

"I'll run both ways."

"And Edmund," Sis said, drawing the blanket more tightly about her shoulders, "if Aunty does come back while you're gone, I promise I'll say it was all my idea. I'll say I hounded you out."

"You may tease," Edmund said solemnly, "but it's not right to leave you alone."

Sis tried to keep from smiling. "Mustn't worry. I'll be a perfect lady and sit quietly reading 'Hansel and Gretel' again and I won't ever stop until you come back. There! Does that make you feel better?"

Before he changed his mind, Edmund went out the door. Once in the hall he put the key in the lock and turned it.

"The door is locked!" he called.

"And I'm safe," he heard her say. "Now, just hurry!"

Clutching the key in one hand, the coin in the other, Edmund scurried down the steps.

In the cold outside, not a soul stirred. Decrepit buildings three and four stories high appeared to teeter over broken sidewalks and narrow, muddy streets. The stench of garbage thickened the dismal air. The only light was the occasional blue blur of candles behind dirty windowpanes.

Edmund kept telling himself that it was wrong to leave Sis. Hadn't Aunty warned that this city was full of danger for them? But then, they did have to eat. And Sis was right: Aunty was always saying things were dangerous.

Oh, why was it so hard to know what to do? Because I'm young, Edmund answered himself. Grownups know what's right. Then he thought, If only I were older and a real man!

An aching isolation filled him. *Where was Aunty?* What could have kept her away so long? When no answers came, he bucked himself up to be brave, then began running.

The saloon on Wickenden Street was a small, dirty place, reeking of soured rum. Two low-burning oil lamps shed dim light, and in the corner a rusty iron stove offered more smoke than heat. The only decoration was a hodgepodge of posters and public bills on one wall. Two tables meant for customers were deserted.

But behind the counter was a burly bear of a man. Bearded, he wore an ill-fitting dinner jacket, and a tilted stove-pipe hat on his head. A pile of old newspapers lay before him.

Edmund made his way to the counter. The man looked down. "Yes, boy," he said gruffly. "What do you want?"

"Please, sir," Edmund whispered. "I'd like some food."

"I've meat pies," the man growled. "And bread. How much money do you have?"

Edmund put down his coin.

After studying it with a baleful eye the man scooped the coin up. From below the counter he pulled out a loaf of bread, cut it in two, wrapped one half in a sheet of newspaper, then handed the package to Edmund. "There you are," he said.

Edmund's heart sank. "Is that to be all?" he asked.

"You're lucky to get that," the man told him.

"Thank you, sir," Edmund mumbled. Relieved that he had at least found them something, he raced out.

He was still running when he turned into Ann Street.

"Here! Boy!" came a cry.

Edmund stopped and looked about. Across the way he saw what appeared to be a very old man. He was quite bent over, covered with a coat and scarf which he'd wrapped around his face against the cold. Only his eyes and white hair could be seen. One hand held a cane.

"Would you help me, boy!" the stranger cried in a pitiful, shaky voice.

Edmund approached timidly. "Yes, sir. What's the matter, sir?"

"I've lost my way."

"Where might you be going, sir?"

"Shamrock Street. Is it that direction?" The man pointed to the right.

"No, sir," Edmund said. "It's quite the other way."

"I'm all confused," the man said with a shake of his head. "It's my eyes. My age . . . Would you be charitable and guide me there?"

Edmund looked toward the tenement where he knew Sis was waiting.

"I'm an old man," the stranger begged piteously. "And cold. I'll perish if I don't find my way!"

Shame filled Edmund. He could hear his Aunty Pru saying how wicked it would be to refuse such a request. He had done wrong in leaving Sis. He knew that. But having done so, he must now do the right thing. He must. "Very well, sir," he said, pocketing the door key. "I'll show you."

"Bless you, boy. Bless you . . ."

Edmund drew close. The man reached out and clutched his arm.

"This way . . ." Edmund said.

"Thank you. Thank you."

They began their walk, the man maintaining a tight grip as though fearful the boy might bolt.

A journey which Edmund could have accomplished in five minutes dragged out to twenty and sorely tried his patience. More than once he reminded himself that to help such an old man was the proper thing. He only hoped Sis wasn't worrying.

At last they reached the corner of Shamrock Street.

"This is it," Edmund announced.

"Thank you, boy. Thank you," the man murmured. Without a backward glance he moved away.

For a moment Edmund watched the bent and white-haired figure disappear into the dark. Then, recollecting himself, he raced back to Ann Street, up the steps to the top floor of the building, then down the hallway. Reaching their room, he tried to open the door. When it didn't give, he remembered he'd locked it. It was the work of seconds to get the key out, insert it in the keyhole, twist, and throw the door open.

With horror Edmund stared into the room. Sis was not there.

PART ONE

PART ONE

1

MIGHT I KNOW YOUR NAME?

THE OLD CITY lay dark and cold. A raw wind whipped the street lamps and made the gas flames hiss and flicker like snake tongues. Fingers of shadow leaped over sidewalks, clawing silently upon closely set wooden houses. Stray leaves, brittle and brown, rattled like dry bones along cold stone gutters.

A man, carpetbag in hand, made his way up College Hill, up from the sluggish river basin, battling the steep incline, the wind, and his own desire. He was not big, this man, but the old army coat he wore — black and misshapen, reaching below his knees — gave him an odd bulk. His face was pale, his mustache dark, his mouth set in a scowl of contempt. Beneath a broad forehead crowned by a shock of jet black hair, his eyes were deep, dark, and intense.

Sometimes he walked quickly, sometimes slowly. More than once he looked back down the hill, trying to decide if he should return to the warm station and the train he had just left. There were moments he could think of nothing better. But he had traveled all day and was exhausted. What he wanted, what he needed, was a place where he could drink and sleep.

And write. For the man was a writer very much in need of cash. A story would bring money. But of late he had been unable to write. Idea, theme, characters: he lacked them all.

Short of breath, he reached Benefit Street. There, he stopped beneath a lamp post and looked south. The porch lamp of the Unitarian Church was glowing, indicating that its doors were open to the homeless. If he had no choice he knew he could sleep there. But his gaze turned north. That was where he wanted to go.

Opening his carpetbag he rummaged through clothing, bottles, a notebook, until he found a letter. He read it. Though he himself had written the letter many times, he still found it unsatisfactory. Still, he felt he'd best deliver it before he changed his mind.

More slowly than before, the man walked north along Benefit Street until at last, seeing the house where he intended to leave the letter, Number Eighty-eight, he paused. The door to the dark red building — ordinary a moment before — now appeared to him like a gaping, hungry mouth. He felt suddenly that he was looking *through* the mouth to a graveyard situated just behind.

Despite the bitter cold, he began to sweat. Pain gripped his heart. He felt as if a million needles were pricking him.

14

Against his agony he shut his eyes until, unable to bear it, he turned and fled. Even as he did someone flung himself from the darkness, crashing into him, and all but knocked him to the ground.

Gasping for breath the man attempted to see who had attacked him. Seeing no one, he was seized with terror. A demon had struck. Then he saw: sitting on the pavement, equally stunned, was not a demon, but a boy.

The man drew himself up. "That," he managed to say, "was a vicious blow."

"I didn't see you, sir," Edmund whimpered. "I'm very sorry."

"I should think you would be," the man said as he brushed off his greatcoat. "You could have sent me to the grave." With a quick step he started off, only to stop. Something about the boy's wretchedness had touched him. And when the boy shivered — he was wearing little more than a shirt and trousers and even these were ragged — the man came back.

"Are you all right?" he asked.

Edmund was too frightened to say.

"I asked you a question," the man said, his voice turning harsh.

Edmund attempted to reply but gave up. Instead he buried his face in his arms and began to sob.

The man knelt. "What are you doing here at such an ungodly hour?" he demanded. "Why have you nothing warmer to wear? What *is* the matter?" He drew up Edmund's face. When he saw how dirty, red-eyed, and streaked with tears it was, he softened. "Why are you so troubled?" he asked.

"She's gone," Edmund blurted out, trying to knuckle the tears from his eyes.

"Who's gone?"

"Sis."

"Sis?" the man repeated in a shocked whisper.

"My sister," Edmund explained, not noticing the strange look which had come into the man's face.

"Gone . . . where?"

"I don't know." Edmund began to sob again.

"Your mother? Your father?" The question was asked with new urgency. "Where are they?"

"I don't have a father, sir. Nor a mother."

The man stared fixedly at the boy. "How long," he whispered, "have you been without them?"

"My mum left a year ago," Edmund answered.

"And your father?"

"Sir?"

"Your father."

Edmund turned away. "He was lost at sea."

"Then who looks after you?"

"Aunty Pru. And . . . now *she's* been gone three days."

"Three days!"

"Aunty told us to wait. She said she'd come back after two hours, that since I was the man of the family, it was my job to take care of Sis. But though we waited, sir —

16

never budged — Aunty didn't return. It was only when we had no more food that I went out to get some bread. It wasn't far. To the saloon on Wickenden Street. I know I wasn't supposed to leave her, but, sir, there was *nothing* left. And Sis was beastly hungry. I had to. It had been two days!

"I did lock the door behind me. And I *did* come right back. But when I did, though the door was *still* locked, Sis was *gone*. Ever since, I've been searching for her. All over the city. And, sir, I've tried to get help, but no one would give it!" Edmund burst into tears again.

"How old are you?"

"Eleven."

The man stood. "On your feet," he said.

Shivering from nervous exhaustion as much as from the cold, Edmund got up. "Please, sir," he said, "I don't know what to do. Can you help me?"

"Perhaps. Do you know your numbers?"

"Yes, sir. I can read."

The man took his letter from his pocket. "Take this to Number Eighty-eight. Deliver it to a Mrs. Helen Whitman. Can you do that?"

"But my sister . . ."

"The letter," the man snapped. Then, more softly, he added, "Afterward we shall see about you."

Edmund, willing to do anything for even the hope of help, struggled to pull himself together. "Shall I say who it's from, sir?" he asked.

17

"She'll know when she reads it. Go on now. I'll wait for you here."

Edmund dashed down the street. As soon as he went, the man stepped into a shadowy recess. From there he watched the boy reach the door of Number Eighty-eight. Saw him knock. There was no answer. The boy knocked again, then looked around as if seeking advice. Even as he did, a gleam of light appeared behind the glass at the top of the door.

The man's heart began to pound. The door opened a crack. The boy was now talking to someone. A hand — to the man's eyes it had the whiteness of a ghost's hand — reached out, withdrew the letter, and quickly shut the door.

Edmund raced back. But when he returned to the place where he'd left the man, it was deserted. His heart sank.

"Here I am," came a voice.

Edmund whirled.

"Did Mrs. Whitman say anything?"

"I don't know if the lady was Mrs. Whitman, sir," Edmund said. "All she said was, 'Thank you.'"

The man looked toward Number Eighty-eight. A candle appeared in a second floor room.

"She's reading it," he whispered.

"Yes, sir," Edmund said, watching the man with puzzlement. After a moment he tugged on his coat and said, "Please, sir, would you help me now?"

The man fixed his eyes upon Edmund with such intensity

that the boy grew uncomfortable. "Is there," he began, "a story to be made out of this boy's circumstances?"

"Sir?"

"A story about a boy," the man continued so that Edmund realized he was talking to himself. "Full of life, he searches for his parents only to find . . ." Becoming conscious of the boy's stare, the man cut himself off. "Where have you been living?" he asked.

"Near that India Street docks, sir, in Fox Point. Aunty Pru let a room there."

"Might I spend the night?"

"Sir?"

"I need a place to sleep."

"I suppose so, sir."

"Well then, lead me to it."

"But *will* you help me, sir?"

"We shall see. What is your name?"

"Edmund Albert George Brimmer. I prefer Edmund."

"Edmund, then."

"Sir? Might I know your name?"

The man considered, shifted his gaze to Number Eighty-eight as if the answer lay there, then turned back to Edmund. "I am," he announced, "Mr. Auguste Dupin."

"Mr. Dupin," Edmund repeated, fixing the name. "Thank you, sir."

"Come then," Dupin said, "lead the way."

Edmund, full of gratitude, started along the street. Dupin, however, turned back once more to stare at the house. This time he was reminded of a death's-head. He looked again at the boy, who had stopped and was studying him intently.

"Have you asked no one for help?" Dupin inquired.

"I told you, sir, many people. All day. But no one would."

"And you're sure you want *my* help?" Dupin went on.

Once again Edmund became aware of the man's eyes. They seemed so fierce, so penetrating. He was reminded of Aunty Pru's constant warning: he and Sis must be very cautious in their dealings with strangers in Providence. But . . .

"I do want your help, sir," he finally said. "I've no one else."

"I know," Dupin said darkly.

Side by side, the two began to walk.

They had not gone long when the door to Number Eighty-eight Benefit opened and a servant girl stepped out. Sleepy, cold, annoyed at having been summoned from a warm bed, she hurried down the street and up the hill until she reached the Hotel American House. There she left — for immediate delivery — a hastily written note. It read:

Mr. Arnold:
Edgar Allan Poe has come.

2

BENEATH A COLD
NOVEMBER MOON

AS EDMUND LED Mr. Dupin toward his room, the elegant houses along Benefit Street gave way to the much poorer ones of Fox Point. Dupin said nothing. He was too busy thinking how he might best describe the boy. *Sad*. Rather *thin*. Certainly *desperate*. The thought made him wonder if Edmund was desperate enough to shade the truth. Could he trust him? Dupin stole a look at him. Edmund was being very silent.

"Are we close to water?" Dupin asked.

Edmund, starting, looked up. "What, sir?"

"I asked you if we are close to water."

"Just two blocks, sir," Edmund replied. "It's the head of Narragansett Bay, where the coastal ships dock."

"You've been there."

"Yes, sir. My sister and I collect boat names."

"Collect *names?*"

After a moment Edmund said, "We don't have much else to do."

Dupin looked inquiringly at him.

"You see we get tired being in our room all day," Edmund explained. "So when Aunty leaves we go too. Well, actually, it's my sister who insists, and I do need to look after her, don't I? Aunty doesn't like us going to the docks, you see. Says it's dangerous. Aunty says most things are dangerous. But we have made friends there. Do you know Captain Elias? He knows everything about ships."

Dupin frowned. "Could your sister have gone down to the docks when you went out?" he asked.

"She's not supposed to. Not without me."

Dupin frowned. "Did you ask your captain if he'd seen her?"

Edmund shook his head.

"Why not?"

Edmund grew thoughtful, then said, "Aunty says we're not to talk of family things."

"You spoke to me."

"You insisted, sir."

"Perhaps," Dupin pressed, "your sister went in search of you. You said you came right back. Is *that* true? No shop windows to examine? No cats to observe?"

Beneath Dupin's stern gaze Edmund hung his head. "An old man requested help in finding his way, sir."

"Ah!"

"But Aunty Pru says you should always help the old ones. So you see, I *had* to."

"You were detained for how long, Edmund? Be exact. One minute? An hour? Details are crucial. How long was it?"

"I'm not sure," Edmund admitted.

"I thought as much. And you may have neglected to lock the door too."

"I *did* lock the door to our room, sir! She couldn't have gotten out."

"Edmund, *she was not there.*"

"But . . ."

"Show me the dock area."

"Now?"

"Edmund, do you desire my help or not?"

"Yes, sir."

They started off again. Edmund kept stealing troubled glances at the man. After a while he stopped. "Sir," he said, "I truly don't think Sis would have come to the docks. Not without me."

"Why?"

"I've thought it over. I think that after I left, Aunty must have returned, and then together, they went in search of me. Somehow we've missed one another. But now, you see, they're back in the room. Please sir, don't think me ungrateful, but perhaps, if it's all the same, I don't need your help."

Dupin put a firm hand on Edmund's shoulder. "Edmund,

there is a difference between what happens and what we would like to have happened. No, we are almost at the docks and we shall look." He steered the boy on.

They reached the waterfront. The cold November moon — partially hidden by the mist — shed pale light of a gravestone hue. Silhouettes of silent ships, mostly sail, some steam, bobbed gently on the bay. Small waves licked the quay. A buoy bell clanged.

Dupin nodded in appreciation. It was the perfect setting for the story. Then he saw, thirty yards away, two men — one holding a lantern — both staring at something on the dock. "Come along," Dupin said. Suddenly he drew in his breath and stopped.

"What's the matter?" Edmund asked.

Dupin put down his carpetbag. A suspicion about what the men might be studying began to grow upon him. "Wait here," he said.

"Is something wrong?"

"I'm going to speak to those men."

"Sir, I do think it would be better if I returned . . ."

"Stay," Dupin said, slipping off his greatcoat and draping it around Edmund's shoulders so as to keep the boy warm. "And mind my bag." Before Edmund could protest further, Dupin walked away.

As he approached the two men he saw that the one holding the lamp was large and powerfully built. His hands were huge, his face broad, flat, and round, disfigured by a scar on the left cheek. His bald head was fringed with thin hair that touched his collar. On his jacket was a brass star, the emblem of the Providence Night Watch.

With him was a short, ferret-faced, white-haired, older man whose wiry body coiled upon itself in a stoop. His eyes kept shifting nervously.

Dupin was struck by the ugliness of the two. Still, he drew closer. As he did, the man with the star on his chest looked up. "Here's a gentleman," he announced gravely. "Let him see." The white-haired man gave way.

Dupin, his apprehension growing, drew near. In a glance he saw it was a woman who lay on the wharf planks. She was dead, but her eyes were still open and held the unmistakable look of shock. It was as if her last view of the world had been some terrible grief.

Her fair hair spread beneath her like an ornamental Japanese fan. Her soaking dress clung to her thin young body. Streaked with green slime, the ivory garment made her look as if she had been cut from marble.

The vision of destroyed youth and beauty sent a tremor through Dupin. He gasped for breath. His fists clenched spasmodically. His head began to throb and he managed not to faint only when the man with the star grabbed him with quick, powerful hands.

"A ghastly prettiness, sir, now ain't she," the man said.

Dupin continued to stare at the woman. She had, he realized, an unmistakable resemblance to Edmund. "Where was she found?" he managed to ask.

The large man touched fingers to his forehead. "The

Providence Night Watch at your service, sir," he said. "Mr. Asa Throck on duty. It was Mr. Fortnoy here —" he indicated his companion — "who just now pulled her out."

Dupin turned to the white-haired man.

Fortnoy, as though requesting permission, twisted up out of his stoop. Throck gave a sharp, commanding nod. Reassured, Fortnoy gestured toward the bay. "I was just in from my boat," he began, his voice a high whine. "Relieved of my watch. It was the whiteness of her dress floating beneath the prow of a clipper that took my attention."

"Who is she?" Dupin asked.

Fortnoy darted an alarmed look at Throck.

The night watchman grunted. "We've no idea," he said.

Dupin, without his greatcoat, shivered in the chilling damp. He glanced over his shoulder. Edmund was looking toward him. "What will happen to her now?" he asked Throck.

"I've sent for the wagon," Throck replied. "There'll be an inquest in the morning. Then, if no one claims her, off to the pauper's field for burial."

Edmund, waiting nervously, saw Dupin beckon. Reluctantly, he picked up the carpetbag and came forward, puzzled that the three men were watching him so intently.

"Put down the bag," Dupin said.

Edmund did, then drew closer, only to realize that someone was lying on the dock. Frightened, he halted and looked to Dupin for an explanation.

"Do you know who that is?" Dupin said.

Edmund was afraid to move.

Dupin turned the boy to look. "There," he whispered.

Edmund darted a swift glance at the body. The sight made his insides shrivel. Hardly able to breathe, he turned away and leaned into Dupin.

"Your aunt?" Dupin whispered.

Edmund could not speak.

"Is it?"

"It's . . . not . . . her dress. . . ."

"Her face, Edmund, her face."

Edmund, unwilling to look again, pressed his eyes against Dupin.

"Answer."

That time Edmund nodded.

The man with the star stretched forward and touched Dupin's shoulder. "That there your boy?" he asked.

Dupin swung about, putting himself between Throck and Edmund. "We must go," he said, retrieving his carpetbag. With a hand on the boy's shoulder, he led the way from the dock.

"But . . . Aunty," Edmund whimpered, unable to find the courage to look back.

"They will take care of her," Dupin said, giving the boy a gentle push. "Now take me to your room."

Edmund went.

3

STEPS IN THE NIGHT

"THERE'S MY BUILDING," Edmund said. "The door is around by the rear." It was the first time either had spoken since leaving the waterfront. He looked up at Dupin. "Sir, must it be me who tells her?"

"What are you talking about?"

"I'm sure she's returned. I've left the door to our room open. And she'll need to know about Aunty."

"Who must know?" Dupin said.

"Sis."

Dupin stopped so suddenly that Edmund looked up at him. The man's eyes were closed.

"You mean," Dupin whispered, "your sister."

"Yes, sir."

"*Sis*," Dupin said with difficulty, "was the name of my late wife."

"Oh, sir, I had no idea. I am very sorry. . . ."

"You should be," Dupin snapped. After a moment he opened his eyes. "What's the name of this place?"

"Ann Street."

Dupin looked about. There was nothing but dark tenement buildings. "Lead on."

"Thank you, sir," Edmund said, deciding not to ask his question again. Instead he made his way to the back door. "Mind the steps," he cautioned.

At the top of the four flights of dark stairs, the boy opened the door that led to the hall. There, unable to restrain himself, he ran to the far end and flung open the door to his room. "Sis!" he cried.

No one was there.

Dupin pushed by him and at a glance took in the room's meager furnishings. "Do you have a lamp?" he asked. "Some candles?"

Edmund was too numb to reply.

"What about food?" Dupin said, fingering an empty water basin.

Edmund managed to shake his head.

"Hardly a way to receive guests," Dupin said sourly. "Is there a place to buy some at this hour?"

Edmund struggled to rouse himself. "There's a saloon, sir. It's not far. They sell bread and meat pies."

Dupin produced a purse from his carpetbag and after a momentary calculation selected a few coins which he gave to Edmund. "A meat pie for us both. And see if they'll sell you candles. Hurry now. I've not eaten since noon."

"Yes, sir."

"What is it?" Dupin said when Edmund made no move to go.

"Is . . . is Aunty truly dead?"

Dupin turned from the boy's pain. "You saw for yourself."

"Sir . . ."

"What?"

"It wasn't her dress."

"Edmund, your aunt is dead."

"But then, *where is my sister?*"

"I haven't the slightest idea. Now go."

Still Edmund stood, uncertain.

"Go!"

Edmund gripped the coins and went off.

Dupin listened tensely until the boy's steps retreated down the hallway. When he was sure Edmund was gone, he reached for his carpetbag and brought out a notebook as well as pen and ink. Quickly, he scratched out a few words.

Story:
Edmund . . . a boy . . . Missing sister . . . The sea —
bringer of death . . . abandonment. Release/death.

Then he added,

The . . . necessity . . . of death . . . The certainty of death.

The act of writing eased his tension. He read over what he had done. The words gave him a sharp pang of pain. *Why must death always be certain? Could he never escape it? Never think of another ending?* Depression crowded in.

Desperate to quiet the pain of his emotions, Dupin slipped the notebook back into his bag and removed a liquor bottle, pulled its cork, and drank deeply.

Then he stood by the window and looked out. What he saw was as uninviting as everything else he'd so far observed: another miserable building, so close he could lean out and touch its filthy windows. As the liquor took hold his pain gave way to anger. Why was he in such a place? It all made his head ache.

Uneasy on his feet, Dupin returned to the table. After replacing the empty bottle in his bag, he took out another and drank that one off too. Gradually, his headache eased. Drowsiness replaced it. Soon he was cradling his head in his arms and dozing.

*   *   *

Edmund stood just outside his building. A heavy fog had crept in from the bay and made the night more impenetrable than ever. The few candles still burning in windows seemed draped in shrouds. His own emotions were in tatters.

Barely twenty-four hours ago he'd left Sis. How many times since then had he rebuked himself for leaving her. If *only* he had listened to his Aunty's cautions! But now — he sucked in a deep breath — Aunty was dead. Momentarily he closed his eyes. It was too difficult to grasp.

And now there was this man, Mr. Dupin. . . . Would he truly help? Edmund couldn't think it through. He forced himself to set off toward the saloon.

But hardly had he done so when he heard footsteps. At once he stopped and looked about. He saw nothing. Again he moved. Again the footsteps came. That time Edmund thought he saw someone on the far side of the street. When he caught sight of what appeared to be light or whitish hair, his heart gave a tumble. "Aunty!" he cried.

The shape seemed to collapse upon itself and disappear.

Edmund gazed into the fog but could make out nothing more. Then he recalled a fairy tale Sis had read to him, and its notion that the recent dead hovered about their former homes, unwilling to abandon the ones they loved. But Aunty had always said there were no ghosts. With a convulsive shudder, Edmund turned and hurried on.

This time the saloon was not quite so empty. The man behind the counter was the same. But at one of the two tables sat three men wearing coats and jackets against the chill. They were playing cards. Half-filled glasses of rum and water stood before them. When Edmund walked in everyone looked up. All conversation stopped.

Edmund noticed that one of the men was the night watchman from the docks.

He made his way to the counter. The counter man looked

down at him. "Yes, boy," he demanded. "What do you want this time?"

"Please, sir," Edmund said, dumping Mr. Dupin's coins on the counter, "a meat pie. And candles."

"Large pie or small?"

"This is the money I have, sir."

The man made a slow count of the coins. "Two candles and a small pie," he said, taking up the money. From a cabinet he fetched candles and matches. From a box behind the counter he retrieved a crusty pie, dusted it, laid it down on his pile of newspapers, wrapped everything up, then thrust the package into Edmund's hands. All the while he gazed at him as if he were some curious bug.

"Thank you, sir," Edmund said and started out.

As soon as Edmund left, the counter man leaned toward those at the table. "Is *that* the boy?" he asked. "The one you was just talking about?"

"The same," Throck returned. "Here from England only a while. Now it's his aunt what got drownded." The card game resumed.

In moments the door opened again. Fortnoy entered. His thin face was protected against the cold by a high coat collar and a muffler.

Throck turned. "Well?" he demanded.

"The boy came directly here," Fortnoy informed him, "then headed right back. Nothing else."

"And the other?"

"As far as I can tell, still there."

"Did the boy see you?"

"For a moment I thought he did. But I stepped away."

Disgusted, Throck flung his cards down and, with hardly more than a farewell glance at his companions, left the saloon with Fortnoy.

"What's the matter with them?" said one of the men at the table.

"Don't you know what he's been working on?" said the counter man.

"He said nothing to me."

"I'll show you," the counter man said. He crossed the room to the wall of bills and posters. "Here," he said, and read from a bill:

"REWARD
Persons providing information leading to the
finding of one Mrs. G. Rachett, of London,
England, but believed to be a recent resident of
Providence, Rhode Island, shall be entitled to a
bonded reward. Please contact Mr. Poley,
Providence Bank, South Main, at earliest
convenience.
Oct. 15, 1848"

One man at the table snorted. "Makes you wonder which part of the law Mr. Throck practices, doesn't it?"

"Well," offered the other, "bread'll take butter on either side."

*   *   *

Edmund, carrying the meat pie and candles, burst into the room. "Mr. Dupin! I got . . ." Dupin was asleep, slumped over the table, empty bottle in hand. A stench of liquor filled the air. "Mr. Dupin," Edmund said again. There was still no response.

Edmund lit a match, let wax drip, fastened the candle on the table, and unwrapped the package. Then he gave Dupin a slight shake. "Mr. Dupin . . ." Dupin continued to sleep.

Feeling the pangs of hunger, Edmund broke the pie in half. To his dismay one piece was slightly bigger than the other. He set the larger portion down on the table. Then he paused and studied the sleeping Dupin. Suddenly, he reached out and exchanged the pieces, taking the bigger one for himself. Sitting on the bed he devoured it in a few bites.

Once he had eaten, his misery returned. Why had his aunty been killed? And where was his mother? Was she even alive? Aunty had insisted they believe that she was. But now . . . ? And Sis, *where was she*? And what would become of him? Would *he* be killed? If he did live who would take care of him?

Edmund listened to Dupin's labored breathing, and again asked himself if this man would truly help. He'd been glad of his providential kindness. Still, he couldn't deny there was something odd about the man. Was it Mr. Dupin's hesitation when he had asked his name? His sudden changes of mood? His drinking? Drinking, Aunty said, was evil. Edmund sighed. Aunty objected to so much. He could almost hear her voice: *Adults can be trusted to take care of children. Children must never question adults. Adults know best. Mr. Dupin is an adult.*

Edmund stole a guilty look at Dupin. There was the business of his stepfather, which he had not told him. But how could he reveal such a thing to anyone? Aunty had called it shameful.

Then the most painful question of all returned — where was his sister? Even as he asked it, answering it now this way, now that, Edmund sank into a fitful sleep.

As Edmund slept the sound of footsteps echoed in the hall. Dupin opened his eyes.

"Who's there?" he called out. All he saw was a candle before him with its small, blue, sputtering flame.

Dizzy, confused, Dupin leaned back in his chair and stared at the ceiling. It was crisscrossed with crack lines, alive as a nest of vipers, creating fantastical shapes and ghastly configurations. In one such nest of lines he saw a death's-head. In another, a pool of blood. In a third, a grave. Wincing, Dupin turned away to stare at the equally marred walls. No images there, just *words*.

"*Poe*," was what he saw first. Then "*Mother*," followed by carefully written letters which spelled out "*Sis*." Finally, inevitably, the word "*Death*" loomed large.

Dupin gave a violent shake to his head. Shivering, he drew his greatcoat over his shoulders and rested his face in his hands. In the close, cupped darkness he knew so well appeared the image of the drowned woman. Now another image: Edmund. As Dupin watched, the skin upon the boy's face tightened, split, and — snakelike — dropped away, leaving only a skull.

Dupin began to sweat. *Death. Always death!* His whole body rocked with pain. Leaning forward, he cradled his head in his arms and sank into a deep sleep. The candle flame grew smaller and at last gutted out.

As darkness descended a piece of paper was slipped under the door. Just as softly, footsteps retreated along the hall, down the stairs and into the mist-drenched night.

4

MEDDLE AT YOUR PERIL!

THIRST, A RAW throat, and a throbbing head woke Dupin in the morning. Painfully he sat up and examined the dreary room. When his gaze fell on Edmund, still asleep on the bed, he had no idea who the boy was.

Bit by bit, Dupin reconstructed the previous night's events, including his half-promise to find the boy's sister. Swearing under his breath, he berated himself for even considering the business. There were more important things to attend to: his courtship of Mrs. Whitman, the need to raise money for his new journal, the desire to write about . . .

Vaguely, he recalled his notion that what was happening to the boy could be a story. He had even made notes. He groped for his carpetbag, relieved to find it by his feet. Then, finding his notebook, he turned the pages and read what he had written. It made his head ache.

Feeling panicky, he rummaged through his carpetbag but found all his bottles empty. His headache intensified. His mouth felt as if it were full of sand.

He looked about again. This time he noticed the half meat pie partially wrapped in newspaper. With a voracious appetite he reached for it.

As Dupin ate he poked idly at the scrap of paper. It was the first page of the *Providence Journal* and contained a column of personal notices from two weeks before. With a mind given to the automatic habit of reading, he casually examined it.

NOTICE EXTRAORDINARY

As this is the season when Game and Oyster
Suppers are in great demand, particularly so as the
Presidential Election is shortly to be decided, we
would recommend those who have suppers
depending, to make arrangements with FRANK
FOSTER, in season, that he may be able to
accommodate all.

NOTICE

Mr. William Arnold is resident in the Hotel
American House on Congdon Street, and is ready
to conduct business with interested parties.
Principals only.

POSITION WANTED

The advertiser, R. Peterson, a good copyist and
accountant, thoroughly discreet, being at leisure
from 6 to 9 P.M. would like any remunerative
employment three or four evenings a week. Apply
at Providence Bank office for particulars.

Bored, Dupin pushed the paper aside. Then stiffly — for
the damp, cold air had chilled him — he drew his greatcoat
over his shoulders, opened the door to the room and looked
out. The foul-smelling, deserted hallway filled him with
self-loathing.

He made up his mind. He would leave. Attend to his own
affairs. Find something else to write about. But as Dupin
stepped back into the room to fetch his carpetbag, he caught
sight of a piece of paper on the floor. He picked it up. It read:

MEDDLE AT YOUR PERIL!

Dupin reread the note. He was being challenged. Insulted!
He looked at the still-sleeping boy. Perhaps, he told himself,
there was more here than the squalor of the place suggested.
Dupin stuffed the note into a pocket and looked about with
new interest.

But the room was so small, so barren, that his energy
quickly flagged. He *would* go. He snatched his carpetbag
and was turning toward the door when Edmund woke.

"Mr. Dupin," the boy asked, "did my sister come back?"

Dupin, embarrassed to have been caught sneaking away, shook his head. He leaned against the window casement and stared out, wondering if Edmund had been feigning sleep and watching him.

"Mr. Dupin," Edmund said, "when I came back last night, you were asleep."

"No doubt."

"I ate only half the pie."

"The larger half."

Edmund blushed. "Sir . . ."

"What?"

"Will you still help me?"

Dupin gazed sullenly out the window, wishing to avoid Edmund's watchful look. Should he or should he not help the boy? Was there, or was there not, a story here? If there was, he needed more information.

"I have," Dupin said at last, "an appointment of great importance this afternoon. Until then I shall spend my time in search of your sister."

"Thank you, sir."

"But let me impress one thing upon you . . . Edmund — if I remember your name," Dupin continued. "It is *you* who have the knowledge that will enable me to resolve this affair."

"*I* do —"

"But though you have these details — only I have the ability to understand them. Therefore, I will need to ask you some questions."

"Yes, sir."

Dupin pulled pen and ink bottle from the carpetbag, opened his notebook, settled at the table, and with pen poised, said, "How long have you — your aunt, your sister, and yourself — lived in this place?"

"Sir . . . ?"

Dupin looked up.

"Is it necessary for you to write out what I say?"

Dupin stared hard at Edmund. "Do you or do you not wish my help?" he asked.

"I do, sir," Edmund answered faintly.

"Then answer *my* questions. How long have you been living here?"

"About a month."

"And you are from England."

"London, sir."

"What brought you here?"

Edmund said nothing.

"Did you hear my question?"

"I did, sir."

"Then answer it."

Edmund took a breath. Finally he said, "A while ago my mum went away and left us with Aunty — that's my mum's sister." Edmund swallowed hard, then continued: "Aunty told us that we were to come to America" — he lifted his eyes — "to try and find Mum."

"When did your mother leave?"

"A year ago."

"And why?"

Casting his eyes down, Edmund said, "I don't know, sir."

"Do you expect me to believe you?"

Edmund hung his head.

Dupin said, "I'll try another way. What made your aunt think your mother was here?"

"She received a message."

"A *message*?"

Edmund nodded.

"From whom?"

"My mother."

"Who brought it?"

"A sailor."

"A friend? A relation?"

"Aunty said he was a stranger."

"And the message said . . . ?"

"I don't know," Edmund whispered.

Dupin sighed. "Edmund, you told me your aunt spent her days out. I presume she was looking for your mother. Did she ever say she'd found her?"

"She would have told us."

"Were you planning to go back to England?"

"Only when we found Mum."

Dupin pointed his pen at the trunk. "What's in there?"

"My aunty's things."

"Have you seen inside?"

"There's only clothing. And some family pictures."

"Do you have a key?"

Edmund shook his head. "Just Aunty."

"Your sister, how old was she?"

"Not *was*, sir. *Is*. She's alive. I know it!"

"Perhaps. How old?"

"Eleven."

"The same as you?"

"She's my twin."

"Twin?"

"It runs in the family."

"Is there anything else you wish to tell me?"

Edmund turned away. "No, sir," he said.

Dupin again put down his pen. "Edmund," he said, "you must trust me."

"I do, sir."

"Then tell me something I can use."

Edmund blushed. Trying to find a way to be helpful he said, "Sir, a few days ago, before my aunty disappeared, she said she was going to meet a man who might help her."

"Did she say who?"

"No."

"Or why she was to meet him?"

"Sis and I believed it had something to do with finding our mum."

"You recall nothing more than that?"

"She was nervous about it."

"With reason. Last night," Dupin continued, "you told me that when you left your sister in search of food you locked the door to this room. Are you absolutely certain you did lock it?"

"I'm sure, sir."

"How many keys are there?"

"Two, sir." Edmund took the key from his pocket and offered it. "When Aunty would go out she'd leave one with us in case we had to go to the loo."

"Loo?"

"Privy. It's behind the building."

Dupin took the key. "Edmund, I shall step out into the hall and lock the door. Just as you said you did. When I do, you will attempt to open it from the *inside*. Is that understood?"

"Why?"

"Edmund!" Dupin cried. "Do you have anyone else to help out?"

"No, sir."

"Then cease your questions and do as I tell you!" Edmund bit his lip. "Yes, sir," he said.

From the hallway Dupin locked the door. "Now," he called in, "try to open it."

"I can't, sir. It won't give."

Dupin unlocked the door, entered the room, strode over to the window and lifted the sash. Damp, cold air rushed in. Leaning out as far as he could, he all but touched the window on the building across the way. Abruptly, he gathered his greatcoat and called, "Come along."

Edmund sprang up and followed.

On the street, the fog from the bay made it hard to see more than a few yards. Even so, Dupin studied

Edmund's building intently, then examined the one to its left.

"Notice," Dupin lectured, "how alike the two buildings are, how the windows on the first level match exactly. It will be the same above. Edmund, do you know which is your room?"

"The one in the back. On this side. But, sir I don't follow you."

"You claimed you locked your sister in your room."

"I did lock the door. I'm sure I did."

"Unless someone else had a key there was only one other way out: through the window of your room — to the window in the building opposite."

"But . . ."

"Edmund, *think*! How else? Where else?"

It took a moment for Dupin's words to sink in. But the moment they did Edmund leaped forward toward the building, found the steps, and raced up to the fourth floor. There they looked down a long hallway lined with doors, the same as in Edmund's building.

"Which would be your room?" Dupin asked.

"That one," Edmund said, pointing to the last door on the left.

"Good," Dupin said, "but we want the one on the right."

Edmund raced down the hall and banged on the door. No one came. He pounded again.

"Here," Dupin said. "Let me try." And he flung himself forward, shoulder against the door. It burst open.

5

AN OLD MAN WITH WHITE HAIR

"NOTHING'S HERE!" EDMUND cried.

Dupin surveyed the empty room. "Not quite. Look!" He pointed to a wooden plank leaning against the wall near the window through which, just across the way, they could see Edmund's room. "Open the window," Dupin ordered.

Edmund did as he was told. Dupin lifted the plank and maneuvered it so it reached from one window to the other. It made a perfect walkway.

"There," Dupin said. "Your sister walked from room to room."

Edmund turned to Dupin with astonishment. "But why?"

Instead of answering, Dupin bent over and began to examine the floor. Suddenly he stood up, quelling a headache with a hand to his forehead. "Edmund, search the floor. See if you can find anything. I need more proof."

"Proof of what?"

"Must you question everything?" Dupin cried. "Just search!"

As Dupin watched, Edmund looked about the floor. Sure enough, in moments he found a pearl button. He snatched it up and brought it to Dupin. "It's from one of my sister's shoes," he explained excitedly. "She's very fond of the shoes. Thinks them very ladylike."

"Any notion as to why she might have left it?"

"Hansel and Gretel!" Edmund said promptly. Dupin looked puzzled.

"It's a fairy tale Sis loves to read," Edmund explained. "About a girl who leaves a trail of crumbs to get back home to her father."

"Then, you see," Dupin said, "I was right. She was here."

"Sir, I still don't think Sis would have come over."

"Not on her own. Of course not. She was forced."

"Do you mean *stolen*?" Edmund asked, wide-eyed.

"Precisely."

"But who would do such a thing?"

"Find the one who did it," Dupin returned, "and we have gone a long way toward solving this mystery. But quickly now."

Before Edmund could absorb what he'd been told, Dupin rushed out of the room. Edmund hurried to keep up with him.

At the main entrance of the house, Dupin yanked hard on the doorbell ringer.

In moments a thin, elderly woman, her gray hair

wrapped high in turban fashion, came to the door. Though she was standing directly in front of Dupin she looked this way and that as if she were blind. "What is it?" she demanded.

"The landlord if you please," Dupin said.

"Is it a room you'll be wanting?" the woman asked.

"Not at all," Dupin said. "I'm a city officer and wish to make an inquiry."

Edmund, surprised by this declaration, looked up at Dupin.

"We have no troubles here," the woman said, making an effort to shut the door. Dupin thrust his foot against it.

"Here," the woman objected, "I'm an old woman that sees but poorly. I've got my rights!"

"We merely wish the name of one of your tenants," Dupin said briskly, as he insinuated himself past the edge of the door. "Fourth floor. Back room. Right-hand side."

"That's none of —" the woman began to say, but she stopped. "That man owes me a week's rent," she exclaimed.

"Exactly. Tell me about him," Dupin said.

"He came here about two weeks ago," the woman went on, now quite willing to talk. "Offered to take a room, and, mind, very particular *which* room. But then, you know, he never lived in it. Just came now and again to pace it out. With another man. Said he was having trouble getting his goods removed. I didn't care. Not as long as he paid. But then, he only gave for the first week."

"His name!"

"He wouldn't give it at first but when I insisted he said it was Mr. Smith."

"And the way he looked?"

The woman shook her head. "A large man. I've not the eyes to tell you more. What are you asking for?"

"A private matter," Dupin said. "Can you tell us anything else about him? It's urgent."

"Urgent?" the woman echoed. "He owes me money. That's urgent."

Dupin let her shut the door.

Edmund tugged at Dupin's coat. "Sir," he said, "are you really an official?"

"Of course not! Is there a place nearby where we can get something to eat?"

Edmund nodded.

"Does it sell drink?"

"Yes, sir."

"Find it, Edmund. Find it!"

*   *   *

It was a large, well lit café, crowded and noisy, that Edmund led them to. Dupin quickly took a table and told the boy to sit. "First," he said, "we shall eat. Then I intend to get you some warmer clothing." He turned to study the chalkboard menu.

As he did, Edmund fell into thoughts about what Mr. Dupin had said, that his sister had been stolen. The notion astounded him, terrified him. His own sister . . . He looked up. Mr. Dupin was staring across the room. Edmund followed his gaze. Mr. Throck, the night watchman, had just entered and a crowd was gathered about him, listening as he talked with animation.

Edmund turned back to Dupin. "Sir . . . ?"

Dupin's eyes remained on Throck.

"Mr. Dupin?" Edmund tried again in a whisper. "Was the person who murdered my aunt the one who stole my sister?"

"What makes you sure your aunt *was* murdered?" replied Dupin, his eyes still on Throck. "It might have been an accident."

"I'm not certain," Edmund admitted, "but . . ."

"Then wait for the facts. Now, I wish to ask *you* something. Were you and your sister together *all* the time until that moment you left her to go for food? Think hard now. It's important."

"I never left her. I wouldn't. And I only did it because . . ."

"Edmund, I'm not interested in *your* reasons. The point being, it's logical to suppose that — if you are telling the truth —"

"Mr. Dupin . . ."

Dupin waved Edmund's objection aside and rushed on, "— then the man who occupied the room opposite yours was waiting, watching for the moment when you *did* leave her alone."

"Watching *us*?" Edmund said, startled.

"Didn't you say that when you went out for food that night you were detained on the street?"

"An old man asked for some help."

"Not just any old man, Edmund. But could it have been . . . an old man with *white* hair?"

Edmund's mouth dropped open. "How did you know?" he said.

"Edmund, that ghastly woman stated that the large man who rented that room had another with him, did she not?"

Edmund nodded.

"Therefore," Dupin said triumphantly, "we are looking for *two* men. While you were out in search of food *and* detained, 'Mr. Smith' — that name is, I assure you, a false one — stole your sister. Furthermore, the appointment your aunt had — from which she did not return — was with one of those two. It was a conspiracy to lure your aunt away so you would be alone with your sister. Then, once you left her . . ."

"Sis told me to go . . ."

". . . they detained you," Dupin rushed on, paying no mind to Edmund, "and stole her *through* the window so as to make certain they would not be observed.

"Who are these people? You said your aunt came to Providence after receiving a message from your mother. A *message*, Edmund, not a letter. This was brought, moreover, by an ordinary sailor, a most casual means of communication. It suggests your mother acted under duress, on the impulse of sudden opportunity. In short, Edmund, the people your mother was consorting with, the man your aunt went to meet and who *perhaps* killed her, the ones who stole your sister – *they are all one and the same.*"

"Do you know who they are?" Edmund said, awed by all that Dupin had deduced.

"I have a good idea." Dupin glanced quickly at Throck.

Before Edmund could ask more, a waiter approached. "Your order, sir?" he said.

Dupin checked what money he had, then requested soup and bread for Edmund, drink for himself. But as the waiter turned to leave, Dupin called him back. "That man over there," he said, "is that Mr. Throck?"

The waiter looked over his shoulder. "It is, sir, and he's got himself a ripe story to tell."

"A murder?"

The waiter shook his head. "Sure now, sir, haven't you heard about the bank?"

"What bank?"

"The Providence Bank. It was robbed last night of California gold. Taken right from the vault like magic. You ask Throck. He'll tell it to you fine." The waiter scurried off.

For a moment Dupin continued to gaze at Throck. Then he took a small notebook from his pocket and began to write in it.

"Sir," Edmund said, "if you aren't an official, shouldn't we inform the authorities that my sister was stolen? You might tell them all you've discovered, mightn't you?"

Dupin kept writing.

Not sure he had been heard, Edmund leaned across the table and touched Dupin's arm. Dupin jumped as though pinched.

53

"What do you want?" he snapped.

"It's about my sister . . ."

"What about her?"

"Shouldn't we inform the authorities?"

"Edmund, I shall say this but once more: If you desire someone else to help you, find him and leave me in peace! So, make up your mind. Is it to be me? Yes or no?"

Edmund sat frozen.

"There," Dupin continued with a nod of his head, "is a member of the Providence Night Watch. Mr. Throck. He would be delighted to lend assistance. But I can assure you, Edmund, *he* will be of very little use. Now, again, do you or do you not wish to learn what happened to your sister?"

"I do, sir."

"Then believe me. Only Auguste Dupin can help you." He smiled faintly. "I may have discovered *how* she was stolen but I do not yet know *why*, much less her present condition. I'll act only when *I* have completed *my* investigations."

"But . . ."

"No buts. Now," Dupin continued without pause, "as soon as we're done here, I've an errand for you to run. In the meanwhile do you know a clothier in the neighborhood?"

"I think so," Edmund said, trying to keep up with Mr. Dupin's constant shifts.

"Good," Dupin said. "No more idle chatter. Here's your soup. Eat it. You're in need."

Afraid to say anything, Edmund turned to the food the waiter had set before him. Mr. Dupin, he noticed, had put the notebook away and was sipping from his glass. But mostly he was keeping an eye on the night watchman. Edmund realized that the man was returning Dupin's stare.

"That clothier you spoke of," Dupin said abruptly. "Is it far?"

Edmund shook his head.

"Good," Dupin said. "Go and determine the price of a coat for yourself. Can you do that?"

"Now?" Edmund said. He had not finished eating.

Dupin checked his pocket watch. "It's nine-thirty. Return in half an hour. Not a moment sooner. Go on. Quickly now!"

Edmund rose from the table, bread in hand, and glanced across the room. The night watchman had come to his feet too.

"Are you or are you not going to do as you've been told?" Dupin pressed.

"Yes, sir. I will." Edmund left the café reluctantly. Even as he did, Throck crossed the room and approached Dupin.

6

THE PROVIDENCE NIGHT WATCH

"DID YOU WANT words with me?" Throck demanded.

Dupin gestured to Edmund's empty seat.

"Don't mind if I do," Throck said, sitting heavily. "I've had a long night."

The two men looked at one another. After a while Dupin said, "It's the officers' fault."

"I've always said so," Throck replied, only to turn red in the face. "Here," he demanded, "how do you know what was in my mind?"

Dupin clasped his hands before him and sat back in his chair. "A matter of observing details, Mr. Throck," he said. "Details.

"You come over here, and you sit down wondering why I have been fixing my attentions on you. You even study me, brow furrowed, trying to guess who I am. I follow your eyes. Your gaze passes from my face to my hand. You can make nothing of that. You notice my coat. That you recognize. You know it for an army coat. I know because the lines on your brow relax. How do you know? Why, *your* jacket is army issue too, which suggests that you, like me, were once in the army. That scar on your face suggests more, as does the pistol you have not quite concealed in your vest pocket."

Without thinking, Throck touched his jacket.

"In short, you enjoy violence to a considerable degree," Dupin continued. "But why should a man like you be cashiered from the army? Here I hazard a guess: you were thrown out for excessive brawling.

"Ah, but if you hadn't been, you'd be in Mexico. Now Mexico, to be sure, is a warmer place. You'd much rather be there. Whose fault is that? It's the officers' fault. I share your opinion of them."

Throck studied Dupin. "Who told you all that?"

"I told you, I notice details. And I believe," Dupin hurried on, wishing to take advantage of Throck's confusion, "that we met along the docks last night. And your friend, Mr. Fortnoy, too."

Throck's eyes narrowed. "Never mind who are my friends and who aren't," he said. "I thought you were interested in that robbery."

"Should I be?"

"Suit yourself."

"What I *do* want to know," Dupin said, leaning forward, "is if any more information has been found about that unfortunate woman pulled from the bay."

Throck studied Dupin carefully. "Don't know what business it is of yours," he said. "'Course," he added, "there's that boy you were just sitting here with. Same as last night."

"What about him?"

"He . . . had a mother."

Caught off guard, Dupin frowned. "A mother?"

"But then," Throck added, "so do we all. Or then, perhaps you don't."

Dupin grew pale.

Throck grinned, delighted to have discomforted the man. "Is that what you wanted to ask me about?"

Dupin struggled to regain his composure. "Last night, you mentioned an inquest. Is that today?"

"I'd have thought you could have detailed that out," Throck said mockingly. "But I'll tell you anyway because I care flea eggs for you. It's at the courthouse. Eleven this morning.

"And," he continued, "that boy who was just here — I asked you last night but you wouldn't answer — is he a relation of yours?"

"Relation?"

"Such as his aunt was looking for?"

"The mother?"

Throck winked. "It takes two."

Dupin felt affronted. "What is all this to you?" he demanded.

"It's my business."

Dupin reached into his pocket, found the note that had

been slipped under Edmund's door during the night, and pushed it across the table. "Is this threat part of your business?"

Throck got to his feet. "You can be sure of one thing, mister."

"And that?"

"Once I promise to find someone, it don't matter to me if they're alive *or* dead. And I don't care what money there is. *I* know what's right. I took an oath to that." He thumped the star on his chest. "You remember that," he said, shaking a massive fist before Dupin. "Throck sees it through."

With that, Throck snatched up the note and hurriedly made his way out of the café, pushing people aside as he went.

Dupin watched him go. "It takes two," he murmured, then called to the waiter for more drink. As Dupin drank he began to wonder at the similarities between the boy's life and his own. Both were abandoned boys. Similar first names. Both with lost fathers. For Edmund an aunt who took the place of a mother. Like himself. And, dear to each, someone called "Sis."

Yes, Dupin realized, their situations were very much the same. In fact, only two details were missing for Edmund. A stepfather. A hateful one. And . . . the death of "Sis."

Have I, Dupin asked himself suddenly — have I gone beyond the writing of words? Could I be writing this boy's *life*? But, he continued, if *I* am writing Edmund's story — and it is the same as mine — then it *must* end with the death of *his* Sis. The thought held Dupin, fascinated him, even as it terrified him.

*   *   *

On Wickenden Street, two blocks from the café, Edmund made his way through the fog to a clothing store. Once inside he stood just by the door and looked about, all too conscious of the poor appearance he made in his tattered trousers and shirt.

It was a large store with shelving which reached to the ceiling. Counters were everywhere. Not a surface was without its bolt of cloth. Edmund wished Mr. Dupin was with him. How was he to find the price of anything?

In the center of the room stood a man on a platform trying on a coat. He was quite portly and had a florid face, pink lips, and great whiskers.

Kneeling below him was a tailor with a mouth full of pins tacking up the bottom of the coat. Yet another man, tape measure in hand, was standing off to one side observing the proceedings.

"They say it was millions," the observer said. "All California gold."

The man on the platform grunted.

"I tell you, sir," the salesman continued, "there's no safety. The vault that gold was taken from had massive locks on it. Massive! And not one of them touched, so they say. The gold flew up the chimney so to speak. There, does that look right?"

The portly man turned slightly to look at himself in a

full-length mirror. As he did he noticed Edmund. For a moment he merely stared. Then a flash of panic came to his face. Violently, he swung away.

The salesman looked around. He saw Edmund, then glanced up at his customer. Seeing the man's dismay, he rushed over to Edmund. "We're not giving anything," the salesman shouted, shoving Edmund toward the door. "Out!"

"Please, sir, I only wanted to find the price of a coat."

"None of that cheek," the man cried.

"It's true, sir. It is!"

"Don't you lie to me!" the salesman insisted. *"Out!"* And he all but threw Edmund onto the street.

Deeply humiliated, Edmund started down Wickenden but recalled Mr. Dupin's admonition not to return too soon. His sense of humiliation increasing, he stepped into a doorway and looked back toward the clothier's. To his surprise he saw the portly man rush out onto the street and look up and down as if in search of something.

Hoof beats heralded the coming of a horse-drawn cab. The man jumped forward and hailed it. "Church Street!" he called, and began to climb inside. Just as quickly he changed his mind. Out he leaped, shouting, "Never mind!" to the driver. The next moment he hurried up Wickenden Street and was lost in the fog.

Edmund watched him go, wondering what had happened. Then he realized that the store was now empty of other customers. He had half a mind to go back in again. But his humiliation had been too great. He turned toward the café.

When he arrived Dupin was sitting at the table writing busily. An empty whiskey bottle stood at his elbow. The night watchman was nowhere to be seen. Worried that he had returned too soon, and not wishing to interrupt, Edmund slipped quietly into his seat.

Dupin looked up with cloudy eyes. "Where have you been?" he asked. His words were slightly slurred.

Edmund was taken aback. "You sent me to the store, sir."

"What store?"

"The clothier. To find the price of a coat. Only they chased me out."

Dupin continued to look at him blankly.

Edmund felt even more uncomfortable. It was as if Mr. Dupin didn't know who he was. "Sir," he repeated, "you told me to go."

Dupin made a dismissive gesture. "Never mind," he said. "You are to deliver this." He tore a page from his notebook, folded it over, and held it out. "Eighty-eight Benefit."

"Is that where I delivered the note last night?" Edmund asked.

Once again Dupin's eyes glazed over with incomprehension.

"Last night," Edmund tried, "you sent me there. Don't you remember? It was right after I ran into you."

Dupin said, "I do remember."

"But weren't we going to get me a coat?" Edmund asked cautiously.

"Edmund," Dupin drawled, "I'm not interested in *coats.*

Now mind, you are to put my letter" — he shook it before the boy — "in the hand — *only* the hand — of Mrs. Helen Whitman." His voice had become even thicker.

Edmund took the letter. "Shall I come back when I deliver it, sir?" he asked.

"To this very spot," Dupin said. "I won't budge. Not an inch. Not until you return. And there's another thing," he said, leaning forward.

Pulling back from the stench of liquor, Edmund waited.

"Don't," Dupin admonished, "don't, under any circumstances, give my letter to Mrs. Whitman *unless* she is *completely* alone. Is that clear?"

Edmund nodded.

"Now go."

Disbelieving, Edmund remained seated.

"*Go!*" Dupin suddenly shouted.

Edmund leaped up and turned toward the door.

But Dupin cried out, "Edmund!"

Edmund stopped.

"I . . . I am the man who was . . . is Dupin. I shall bring this . . . story to a satisfactory end. Now, be off!"

Trying to fight the pain in his chest, Edmund turned and went.

As soon as Dupin saw the boy go, he got to his feet and drew on his greatcoat. "Waiter!" he called.

"Sir?"

"Directions," Dupin demanded. "Directions to the courthouse!"

7

JUDGMENT OF MURDER

EDMUND, DETERMINED TO stay on Mr. Dupin's good side so as to keep him looking for Sis, ran most of the way up Benefit Street to Number Eighty-eight. On the steps he went over his instructions, then, still breathless, he knocked on the door.

A servant girl opened it. "Yes, please?"

"Please, miss. I've a letter for a Mrs. Whitman."

"Thank you," the girl said, and reached out.

Edmund drew back, "I was told to give it only to her."

"And who gave you that particular instruction?" the girl demanded.

"Mr. Dupin."

The girl examined Edmund suspiciously. "You're very dirty," she informed him.

Edmund stammered, "I'm only doing what I've been asked, miss."

"If I let you in, will you promise not to touch anything, and make no dirt?"

"Yes, miss. Of course not."

The girl led Edmund into the vestibule. "Stay here," she said, but before she hurried off, she gave him another warning. "Don't you be making a mess, now."

Grateful to be out of the cold but upset at having been spoken to in such a way, Edmund looked beyond the hall where he'd been left. The walls were covered with patterned wallpaper. The floors had carpets. Silver and books were on display. It made him feel uncomfortable to be in a wealthy home.

The servant girl returned. "Come, boy," she said tartly and brought him into a well-furnished room. There, on a chaise longue, a woman was reclining.

Her face was fair, with soft brown eyes. Masses of ringlets reached her shoulders. The splendid silk dress she wore — and which was spread about her — the small book she held in one hand, made her look like a picture. Edmund had never seen anyone so grand.

"Mrs. Whitman," the servant said, "this is the boy who's come."

Mrs. Whitman gazed at Edmund with friendly curiosity. "I'm told," she said, "you have a letter for me."

Edmund, quite overwhelmed, merely nodded.

"But you've been required to place it directly into my hands."

"Yes, ma'am."

"Is it about the afternoon tea Mrs. Powers — my mother — has arranged?"

"I don't know, ma'am."

Mrs. Whitman smiled. "May I have the letter then," she said.

"Please, ma'am," Edmund managed, "I promised to give it only when you were alone."

"Who gave you these romantic orders?"

"Mr. Dupin."

"Who," Mrs. Whitman asked, "is Mr. Dupin?"

Edmund didn't know how to reply.

Mrs. Whitman repeated the name several times. Then suddenly her face became red. "Ah!" she cried. "Catherine, you may go."

The girl gave Edmund what he took to be a frosty look — as if he'd done something wrong — then curtsied to her mistress and left.

Mrs. Whitman smiled nervously. "So it is Mr. Dupin who has sent you."

"Yes, ma'am," Edmund said, increasingly uncomfortable about the confusion his coming seemed to have caused. He wished he could leave.

"Where is . . . Mr. Dupin?"

"In Providence, ma'am."

Mrs. Whitman sat up. "Is he?"

"He had me deliver a letter to you last night."

Her face paled. "Last night?"

"It was very late."

Mrs. Whitman suddenly stood. "Let me have your letter," she said with an air of alarm.

Edmund gave it to her, wondering why she was so agitated. She started to open it, then stopped and hurried to the door.

Edmund was sure she was checking to see if anyone was listening. Satisfied that no one was, she began to open the letter. But again she paused. "If anyone should ask you why you've come," she warned, "tell them . . . it *was* Dupin who sent you."

Further perplexed by this statement of the obvious, Edmund only nodded.

Mrs. Whitman studied the letter for a long time. At last she looked up. "Can you tell me," she asked, "how . . . Mr. Dupin is?"

"He's fine."

A line of worry creased her brow. "Where is he now?"

"In a café on Wickenden Street."

"Is he . . . drinking?"

Edmund looked down at his feet.

"Please. It's *very* important. Was he drinking?"

"A . . . little."

Mrs. Whitman sighed. "Mr. . . . Dupin is a genius. The most passionate, the most romantic of men. But . . ." Suddenly, she stopped. "What is *your* name?"

"Edmund."

"Edmund what?"

"Edmund Brimmer."

"Is that *your* real name?"

"Yes, ma'am," Edmund replied, trying to grasp the meaning of these questions.

"Edmund . . ." she began. A knock on the door interrupted. Mrs. Whitman turned to him. "Not a word about this to anyone!" she whispered urgently. "Do you understand? No one!"

Edmund nodded.

The door opened. It was the servant girl.

"Yes, Catherine?" Mrs. Whitman asked.

"Ma'am, your mother wishes to speak to you immediately."

After a moment Mrs. Whitman said, "Catherine, take this boy down to the kitchen and tell Cook to get him bread and butter. Then ask my mother to join me here." She turned to Edmund. "I will call for you."

Edmund, feeling he had no choice, agreed. Besides, he was hungry.

*　　*　　*

Dupin stood amidst a crowd before the courthouse, gazing at the entrance and waiting for the doors to open. Absentmindedly he rubbed his chin and realized he hadn't shaved. Nor did he feel particularly clean. That annoyed him. He knew he could not go to Mrs. Whitman's looking and feeling as he did. He would have to find a way to bathe.

Dupin wondered anew what had possessed him to take an interest in the boy and his predicament. Was there really a story to be written? The image of the drowned woman came into his mind. She had been, he recalled, quite beautiful.

Was it, he asked himself, her beauty which made her dead? Or was it death which made her so beautiful?

The courthouse doors swung open. The crowd surged forward. Trembling, Dupin went inside.

* * *

In Mrs. Whitman's kitchen, a large black stove bloomed with heat. Edmund, sitting before it, held a slab of bread slathered with jam. Cook had her hands deep in bread dough.

"All that gold," the woman chatted, "and all those men digging it up in far away Californy, then bringing it to Providence where it disappears like so much green mist. Can you imagine, lad, what a body might do with such a pile as that? No pushing bread or delivering messages for you or me. Now *there's* a providence I'd give my heart and soul to! You never do know what will happen next, do you? Well, a prayer for the living, say I."

Edmund ate his bread greedily. "Sis *is* alive," he prayed under his breath. "She *is* alive!"

* * *

Dupin gazed over the gloomy chamber that was the court. The air was close and fetid, the walls streaked with soot, garlanded with dust-clogged webs. A few oil lamps oozed sickly yellow light over a silence stirred just occasionally by the flutter of legal papers.

Spectators were slumped on benches, but it was too dark

for Dupin to see their features. Were they there, he mused, just to avoid the cold? Would any of them pay attention to the proceedings?

Two court officers strolled in. A fat bailiff followed, then came Throck, bold dome of a head gleaming. He was followed by the bent, white-haired figure of Fortnoy, who looked about nervously as though fearful he was entering a trap.

"All rise!" came a cry.

People shuffled to their feet. The judge, black robes draped like a Roman toga about his thickset body, entered. Ponderously, he climbed up to his high seat, then hammered the gavel twice. "State of Rhode Island and Providence Plantations Court of Inquest in session!" he intoned.

"Inquest in the matter of unknown woman found dead in the bay!" chanted a court officer.

The gavel banged again. "Proceed!"

Dupin tried to concentrate on the barely murmured words spoken by now this officer, now that. They didn't seem to care if anyone beyond the judge heard. And the judge, with partly lidded eyes, seemed asleep.

Throck told how he was summoned by Fortnoy. How he had examined the dead woman. How he had called for the police wagon.

Did he know who the woman was? "No."

Fortnoy gave his story. How he served as watchman on the ship, *The Lady Liberty*. How, when relieved of his watch, he had spied the body of the deceased as he rowed to shore. How he had hauled her in.

Did he know who the woman was? "No."

The judge dismissed Throck and Fortnoy. They left.

The talk continued. Endlessly. Waves of tiredness swept over Dupin. Sorry he had come, he struggled to keep his eyes open.

A doctor was called to testify and did so while constantly pinching his nostrils with a hairy hand that muffled his words. Dupin decided he didn't want to hear them. Instead, he tried to study the spectators. One, he noticed, was leaning forward, paying particular attention. Who was it?

His eyes grew heavier. He heard the doctor say, ". . . marks on the throat . . . violence directed against the person unknown, by person or persons unknown, with malice aforethought . . ."

A groan seemed to come from one of the spectators. Who — Dupin asked himself — was making that pitiable sound? Someone cares. That's important. A clue. He strove to regain full consciousness but could not. As he sank deeper into torpor and confusion the vision of the drowned woman loomed up as if *she* herself was in the court observing her own inquest, crying for vengeance.

Dupin pressed his hands to his eyes seeking to dispel the vision. Cries of objections. Cries demanding silence. A bang like the report of a pistol.

A voice called out, "Judgment of willful murder of female unknown by persons unknown for reasons unknown!"

In the darkness which was Dupin's thought — or was it a dream? — he conjured the sound of footfalls, as if the phantom he'd just observed was fleeing the court, light hair trailing like a shroud. Then all became an abyss of dark.

Behind Dupin a hand slowly reached out, moved forward, and grasped his shoulder. A spasm of terror tore through him. Leaping to his feet, he whirled around.

"No sleeping, sir," an aged court officer warned.

Dupin looked about. The court was empty. Other than the officer, he was the only one there. He and a sense of inescapable death.

8

A PERFECT TOMB

EDMUND SAT ON his hands while Cook talked of little more than the bank robbery. He didn't care a thing about that. He preferred to think about Mrs. Whitman. He thought she was kind. Perhaps he could tell her what was happening, even ask her advice about Mr. Dupin. They seemed to be friends.

Before he could make up his mind, Cook finished her bread-making and left the kitchen, telling him that Catherine would soon return. When more time passed, however, and Catherine didn't come, Edmund grew increasingly fretful that Mr. Dupin, waiting in the café, would be anxious about him. He decided he should tell Mrs. Whitman he must leave.

Unsure which way to go, he made his way out of the kitchen and found a closed door. He was about to push it open when he heard urgent voices from the other side.

". . . but when I intercepted that note last night," came a woman's whisper, "I felt obliged to send for you. The man insists upon seeing her. And when you didn't reply . . . I'm so glad I noticed you next door in the cemetery."

"Does *she* know he's coming?" a man's voice answered.

"You may be certain I didn't give her the note."

"But can you put him off?" the man asked.

"We must try," the woman said. "Despite her infatuation, Mr. Poe is totally unsuitable for her. If she is to marry again, you, Mr. Arnold, should be her husband."

"I'm in perfect agreement," the man said. "I'm sure I can provide far better for her, and you."

"All the more reason to act quickly," the woman went on. "Everything must be done to get her to see the truth about him. He plans to call upon her this very afternoon. Naturally, I made it my business to invite other people. They mustn't be alone. You must be here, Mr. Arnold. I'm counting on you to expose him. Reveal him for what he is, an irresponsible drunkard with not a shred of decency."

"Mrs. Powers, I will be only too happy," the man replied. "If he arrives unexpectedly, send Catherine to the hotel."

Their voices drifted away. Edmund wondered who they were and what they were talking about. Expose whom?

Chiding himself that it was, after all, the business of adults and not his, he cautiously pushed open the door. Now he found himself in a little foyer. A scrap of paper lay upon the floor. Not wanting the servant to think he had left it there, he picked the scrap up. And when he did he saw that it had odd writing on it.

988; 98 5; ;48 4‡ ;80 6 45¶8 9‡¶ 8† 36(O 5*† 3‡ O† 9?); 085¶ 8)?*(6)8 5;)6# 59

Even as Edmund tried to make sense of what he read, Catherine burst upon him, "There you are!" she said. "I've been looking all about for you. Quickly now. Madam is waiting."

Edmund hastily shoved the paper into his pocket and followed.

*   *   *

Dupin stood outside the courthouse, taking in great gulps of cold air, his thoughts reverberating with what he had heard: Edmund was right, his aunt *had* been murdered. That thought quickly fused with the fantastical image he'd concocted in the courtroom, the vision of the murdered woman haunting the inquest.

Dupin tried to shake his head clear. The murder was the last thing he needed to think about. If he was to marry Mrs. Whitman he must remain fixed to that purpose, clear-headed, sober. It was drink that deflected him, confused him, he told himself. He put his hand to his heart and swore that he would not drink again. *Ever.*

So resolved, Dupin decided it would do him good to walk briskly back to the café where the boy would be waiting.

As Dupin crossed to the east side of the Providence River, he couldn't help but observe the row of fine buildings directly across the way, snug beneath the bluff of College Hill. One building in particular caught his eye, a brick structure with an unusually graceful gable roof. Drawing closer he realized it was the Providence Bank, the same bank in which last night's robbery had taken place. And on the same night, he noted, that the murder had occurred. Wasn't it Throck who had mentioned all of that? Dupin snorted. Criminals often drew attention to their own criminal acts.

His interest piqued, Dupin studied the building. It was a structure three and a half floors high whose central door — there were not others — was large and flanked by two pillars. To either side were small windows covered with bars. The floors above had five windows each — also barred. Dupin remembered the café waiter saying something about the gold having "disappeared like magic."

Other people seemed to be curious too. Loiterers were hanging about the bank's entrance, a sufficient number to require posting a guard from the regular Providence Police. When Dupin approached, the man held up a hand.

"Sorry, sir. You must have particular business to enter today."

"My name," Dupin announced grandly, "is Auguste Dupin of the Lowell Insurance Company. I have a particular concern in the matters at hand."

The policeman saluted. "Very good, sir," he said, stepping back. "You may pass."

Dupin, watched with curiosity by the loiterers, entered the bank.

*　*　*

When Edmund returned to the drawing room, Mrs. Whitman was alone and standing by a window. From the nervous way she pressed her hands together, he could see she was even more agitated than before.

"Here's the boy, ma'am," Catherine announced.

"Very good," Mrs. Whitman replied, without turning. "You may go."

"Yes, ma'am." As she left, Catherine gave Edmund yet another hostile glance. Again he wondered what he'd done to deserve it.

For a moment Mrs. Whitman remained where she was, staring out the window, Edmund studied her, waiting for the right moment to talk to her about his plight. But the longer she kept her back turned, the greater grew his uncertainty. She appeared so very upset. It seemed hardly right for him to intrude upon her thoughts.

At last she faced him. "Edmund," she began. "I wish to ask you something about . . . Mr. Dupin."

Edmund's heart sank. She seemed so preoccupied with Mr. Dupin — how could his concern about Sis interest her?

"You said that he had been drinking," Mrs. Whitman continued. "A great deal?"

Edmund was not sure how to answer.

"Edmund," she pressed, "I need to know the truth no matter how unpleasant. There . . . there is a possibility — a likelihood — that your friend, Mr. Dupin, and I may be . . ." She paused and shook her head. "I have the greatest admiration for the man and his work. Perhaps you're not aware that *I* write poetry. It was I who reached out . . ." Again she broke off. "Edmund, would you trust a person who drinks?"

It was a question Edmund had asked himself about Mr. Dupin. As for answering, he didn't know what to say. Here was an adult seeking advice from him! He was too startled to speak.

Mrs. Whitman, however, took his silence as an affirmation of her concern. She sighed. "Yes. Even a little is too much. You call him Mr. Dupin. May I ask why?"

The question surprised Edmund. Perhaps Mrs. Whitman and Dupin were not friends after all. . . . Then he recollected that when he first came she seemed to have forgotten the man's name. "It's his name, ma'am."

"You know him by no other?"

"Should I?" Edmund asked, finding the woman as baffling as Mr. Dupin.

Mrs. Whitman bit her lip. "Edmund, how do you come to know him? Are you some . . . relation?"

"We met last night."

"How?"

Without answering, Edmund looked into Mrs. Whitman's troubled face. To answer that question would be to explain

78

his emergency, and he'd already decided he could not do that.

She sighed again. "Very well. I wish you to give him a message."

"Yes, ma'am."

"Tell . . . Mr. Dupin . . . he may come. Not at four o'clock as he proposes, but at three-thirty. And Edmund, tell him . . . not to come to the front door. No, he should go behind the house, to the small graveyard whose entrance is on Church Street. We can meet in privacy. No one ever goes there. Now, repeat what I said."

"Three-thirty behind the house, in the cemetery on Church Street, where no one ever goes."

"Good," she said. "You may leave."

Edmund started for the door.

But she called him back. "You need *not* repeat what I asked you about him. And," she added, lowering her voice, "be advised, the maid, Catherine, works for my mother, Mrs. Powers, not me. Now hurry and deliver my message."

Edmund left her.

*　　*　　*

Dupin walked into the room nearest the bank entrance. Six clerks, all perched on high stools before high desks, were scribbling away on ledger books by the light of gas lamps. At the back of the room — nearest the coal fire — was an older gentleman whose desk, rather like a pulpit, stood higher than the others. When Dupin entered, everyone in the room looked up.

"I am," Dupin said, responding to their inquiring looks, "a private investigator from the Lowell Insurance Company. I've been sent here to examine the place from which the gold was taken."

All heads turned to the rear of the room where the older man was perched. "Mr. Peterson," this man called out, "show this gentleman the vault."

"Yes, Mr. Poley," said the young man closest to the door. He had sprung off his stool when Dupin announced himself.

Dupin turned. Mr. Peterson looked to him to be no more than sixteen or seventeen, the youngest in the room. His eyes were a pert, bright blue. His cheeks were round and red; his hair so blond as to be almost white.

"This way, sir," Peterson called. He'd taken up a candle and gestured to the hall. Dupin followed. From there the young man led the way up a central stairwell which corkscrewed to the top floor.

"Terrible shocking, isn't it?" the young man said as they climbed. "All that gold, gone."

"When did it arrive?"

"A week ago."

"Not a secret I gather."

"Oh no, sir, very much a secret," Peterson replied. "Though not here in the bank. We all knew it was coming. Mr. Poley — he's that older gentleman in charge of the accounting room — he gave orders that not a word should be spoken about it."

80

"Even as he told you."

The young man giggled. "Mr. Poley is a regular chatterer, sir. As open as his ledger. No, he's not one to keep a secret. There was great excitement about the gold being from California. They say it's there for picking off the ground. Do you believe that? Some say yes. Some say no. Here we are, sir."

They had gone up three flights and were now on the top floor. Dupin, panting from the effort, stood before a massive black iron door. It was open wide.

"Did you see this gold arrive?" Dupin asked, eyeing the door as if it were an adversary.

"Not me, sir. Mr. Poley told us it came in the middle of the night. In bar form. Direct from the ship that brought it here. He said it took five men to carry that chest up those same steps we came on."

"Did the gold happen to come from a ship called *The Lady Liberty*?" Dupin asked.

"I can't say that I know. The gold was placed here," said Peterson, nodding to the vault. "You're welcome to look in. But I can assure you, there was not a thing to be found. They had me clean it out this morning myself."

"Not a thing?"

"Well, not quite," said Peterson after a momentary hesitation. "I did find this." He reached into his pocket and held out his hand. A white button lay on it. "Perhaps," he said with a smile, "you can solve the mystery."

Dupin reached into his pocket, felt the button Edmund had found and was about to draw it out when Peterson said, "Go into the vault, sir. Rest assured, I won't lock you in."

The mere idea gave Dupin a turn of nausea. He glanced up into Peterson's smiling blue eyes, then gazed into the vault with discomfort. Tentatively, he took the candle Peterson offered and forced himself to enter.

It was as large as a small room, cold, dark, and empty. And Dupin was struck instantly by how, once inside, he felt completely cut off from the world. He might have been a hundred feet underground rather than — as he knew to be the case — a hundred feet above and snug against the hill. He lifted his eyes. The dancing light of the candle flame created the illusion that the walls were moving in and out, as if he were captive within a beating heart. His queasiness increased.

More and more unsteady, he put a hand to one of the walls. It was hard, clammy. He cringed back and kept to the middle of the room.

"Is there no way in or out save this door?" he asked. His voice produced an answering metallic echo. His breathing became labored.

"Just this," Peterson said brightly, rapping the iron door of the vault. "But they say it wasn't even opened. Tight as a coffin lid. And still, for all that, the gold was taken."

"And the box in which the gold was kept?" Dupin asked. He was growing weaker.

"Perhaps I misspoke," Peterson replied. "There was no box. I was told the gold bars were unloaded outside and carried in, one by one, and placed where you stand. Quite manageable that way."

Dupin, fighting off growing dizziness, looked down. "What's the floor made of?" he asked.

"Iron."

Fearful of total collapse, Dupin knelt to touch the floor's cold surface. When he did he noticed a bit of string. He snatched it up and put it in his pocket, then came unsteadily to his feet. Hands trembling, he held the candle high. Directly overhead he saw what looked like a shaft. It had an opening no more than a foot wide and receded up into darkness.

"And that?"

"An air shaft."

"To the roof?"

Peterson stepped forward to peer up. "I should think so."

"Couldn't the thief have come down through there?" Dupin managed to say, despite the tightness of his throat.

"I doubt it," Peterson answered, taking another look. "It's far too narrow, isn't it? I'm fairly thin myself, but even I couldn't get through."

"Yes," Dupin agreed, laboring for breath, "no grown person could."

"The story," Peterson said, "is that the man who built this vault had a desperate fear of being locked in. That's why he built the shaft. Otherwise a trapped person who might not be rescued for days would perish from suffocation. It *would* make a perfect tomb, now wouldn't it?"

It was then that Dupin fainted.

9

NEWS OF SIS

AS EDMUND HURRIED toward Fox Point he kept thinking about Mrs. Whitman. Why had she asked him so many questions about Mr. Dupin?

Edmund found it all very upsetting, the more so when he realized he had few satisfactory answers himself. He made up his mind that when he reached the café he would ask Mr. Dupin for some.

Dupin was not at the café however.

Merely puzzled at first, Edmund asked the waiter who had served them if he knew where Mr. Dupin had gone.

"Oh, him," the waiter said when Edmund offered a description. "He went off right after you did."

"Right after?"

"He did leave a notebook. You sit down. I'll fetch it."

Edmund, his anxiousness increasing, sat at one of the

tables. In moments the waiter placed the notebook before him.

Edmund gazed at it, wondering what it was that Mr. Dupin had been writing. No, it would be wrong to look. But then, they were *his* answers that Mr. Dupin had put down. He would take just a glance.

Edmund drew the book close and opened it cautiously. On some pages there were just words, like *search* and *death*. Death, he quickly saw, appeared more than any other. And then there were notes which were so rambling and confused Edmund could make no sense of them. But on one page he was able to grasp something. It was headed, *Plot*.

> *Story of a search . . . boy searching for vanished sister . . . wants her to be alive . . . of course . . . no tension there . . . to be effective must be a puzzle . . . is she alive? . . . Enter Dupin . . . Who took her? . . . much confusion . . . but then, boy finds that . . . One can find life only through death. I know. My Sis is dead too.*

Edmund stared at the page, horrified. He recalled Mr. Dupin's questions and his own answers. These lines were much more than that. He reread them. When he reached the word, *death*, that word so often written, he shuddered, closed the book, and pushed it away. There was something very wrong with Mr. Dupin.

But, he asked himself, who else could he turn to? He'd already decided against Mrs. Whitman. He considered the night watchman — Mr. Throck, he thought his name was. He'd seen him at the saloon the night before. Perhaps he could find him there again.

Then he recalled Mr. Dupin's words that only he, Dupin, would be able to find his sister. The next moment Edmund reminded himself that in some magical way Mr. Dupin had figured out that Sis had been stolen. He had even reminded him that on the way back from the saloon he'd met a white-haired man on the street. Perhaps he would find Sis.

"Trust adults," his poor aunty always told him. *"Trust adults."* Edmund sighed. Sometimes it was very hard. Too hard.

*　　*　　*

Dupin was drowning, sinking beneath the bay. Cold water seemed to be pouring into him, gagging him, suffocating him. He wanted air desperately but he was being held by the throat, pushed deeper down. It took superhuman effort to open his eyes, to see who was trying to kill him. It was a man. A man with white hair. It was Peterson, the young accountant, bending over him.

"Sir, are you all right?"

Gradually, Dupin's head cleared. The throbbing eased. With Peterson's help, Dupin sat up and looked about, unsure of where he was. Then he remembered: he was inside the bank vault. Feeling acute embarrassment, he held out a hand. Peterson took it, and helped him to his feet.

"Some fresh air might do you good, sir," the young man suggested. He guided Dupin to the steps. "Hold on to the balustrade. Slowly now."

At the lowest level Peterson paused. "Just a moment," he cautioned and dashed into the office and to Mr. Poley's desk.

"Ah, Mr. Peterson. Did you show that inspector the vault?"

"Yes, sir," Peterson whispered, "but I'm afraid he suddenly took ill."

Mr. Poley became alarmed. "Ill?" he said loudly. The other clerks turned to listen.

"Perhaps," Peterson said, "it would be wise for me to make sure he reaches his lodgings safely."

"Good thought, Mr. Peterson. See that you do. I should be much obliged."

Peterson started off. "Ah, Mr. Peterson!" Mr. Poley cried. The clerk turned. "Your friend, Mr. Rachett, came in and left a message for you." He handed Peterson a folded piece of paper.

Hesitating momentarily, Peterson took the note.

"Go on, sir," Mr. Poley urged. "You'd best take the time to read it. He said it was urgent."

Under Poley's frankly curious eyes, Peterson unfolded the note and read it quickly. When he glanced up he realized everyone was watching him.

"Is something the matter?" Poley asked. "You look stricken."

Peterson jerked around. "No, sir," he said. "Not at all. I'll see to the inspector." Stuffing the note into his pocket, he returned to the hall, relieved to find Dupin still there.

The two emerged onto the street. Dupin, aware that they were being observed closely from the crowd of loiterers, turned from them and took in the fresh air.

"Can I help you anywhere?" Peterson inquired. "I've permission to see you to your lodgings."

Dupin shook his head. "I can make my own way," he insisted.

"To tell the truth, sir," Peterson confided, loath to let Dupin go, "I don't intend to be an accountant forever. I've always wanted to be an investigator like you. I believe I have a good mind for it. I've read a great deal too. Eugène Sue. And Vidocq. Our own Edgar Allan Poe. Have you ever read 'The Gold Bug'? It's very instructive, I think. I'm afraid," he rattled on, "I didn't catch your name when you introduced yourself. Would you be kind enough to give it to me?"

Dupin gazed at him, then said, "Edward Grey."

"Very good, Mr. Grey," Peterson replied, producing a calling card. "Here's mine."

Dupin glanced at the card —

MR. RANDOLF PETERSON
Hotel American House

— and shoved it into a pocket.

"If ever you need someone here in Providence to assist

you in your investigations, Mr. Grey," Peterson pressed, "please call upon me. I'm thoroughly discreet." He held out his hand.

Dupin shook it lamely. "Thank you," he said.

Peterson watched anxiously as Dupin walked away. Then he unfolded the note he had been given by Mr. Poley, and studied it. ". . . at the hotel . . ." he murmured, only to stop when he realized he was talking out loud. Then he hastened up the hill behind the bank.

Two of the loiterers separated from the crowd. One followed Peterson. The second, Mr. Throck, followed Dupin and watched him go into the first saloon he came upon.

*   *   *

Edmund continued to wait in the Wickenden Street café, growing more and more troubled the longer Mr. Dupin was away. Then it occurred to him that perhaps he was the one who had misunderstood. Perhaps Mr. Dupin had gone to the room and was waiting *there.*

He quickly snatched up the notebook, and raced to his building and up the steps. From the hallway he saw that his door was open. He stopped short. His hopes soared. Sis had returned! Down the hall he dashed. . . . The room was a shambles. Everything was scattered. The table was overturned, the chair tossed aside. The trunk had been opened and its contents were spewed about the floor.

Stunned, fighting back tears of anger and despair, Edmund began to set the furniture to rights, then the litter. He turned to Mr. Dupin's belongings — including a shocking number of empty bottles — and put them back into the carpetbag. Finally he collected all that had been pulled from his aunt's trunk.

It was only then that Edmund realized something *had* been taken. Aunty Pru had had a drawing, a portrait of herself and Mum made by a street artist near Piccadilly Circus just before his mother had gone to America. Aunty claimed it was a good likeness of them both and had got the picture up in a little frame. She liked to show it to Sis and Edmund, saying that seeing it helped to keep up one's faith. The drawing, and that alone, had been taken.

To Edmund, it seemed a senseless theft.

Once the room was set to rights he flung himself on the bed and looked about. Now that he was alone, now that he had to confront the fact that he might never see his sister or his aunty there again, Edmund realized how empty, how ugly it was. The very cracks on the ceiling and walls, as if they were some contorted message, seemed to spell out the undoing of his life.

The thought of a message reminded him of the paper he had discovered in Mrs. Whitman's house. He took it from his pocket and once more tried to decipher it. Unable to, he stuck the paper in his sister's book.

His sister's book. Unreadable messages. Ugly, deserted room.

A fist of anger hammered in his chest. "No!" Edmund shouted, "Sis is not dead. She's alive! She is!" Consumed by sudden hopelessness, Edmund flung the book across the room, then hid his face in the blanket. The next moment he was up. He had to find Mr. Dupin.

*   *   *

His drinking done, Dupin proceeded unsteadily toward Wickenden Street. When he reached it he remembered he had wanted to buy Edmund a coat. He entered the first clothing shop he saw.

A salesman approached. "May I help you, sir?"

"A coat," Dupin said.

"Don't move," the salesman exclaimed. In moments he returned holding one. "Beautiful coat, isn't it?"

Dupin looked at it dubiously.

"There's a story behind this coat," the salesman said. "A man orders a coat — not cheap, mind you. He has it fitted and cut for him. He comes in — this morning, actually — for the final fitting. We are trying it on when suddenly, with not so much as a 'by your leave,' the gentleman rushes off, and we have not heard from him since."

The oddness of the event piqued Dupin's curiosity. "No idea what made him go?"

The salesman shrugged. "A boy had wandered in."

"A boy?"

"A begging boy. I'll tell you what, sir. That man never put a penny down. Of course, we took him for a gentleman. Now we've done the work and don't know whether he'll be back or not. Quite a loss for us."

"That begging boy?" Dupin asked. "What time did he appear?"

The man considered. "Between nine-thirty and ten. Now, sir," he persisted, "since we don't know if our customer is coming back, we would be willing to sell you this coat — taking it in a bit — at a considerable saving. That way we wouldn't lose . . . nor would you."

"What did you say this man's name was?"

"I didn't, sir, but I don't mind saying. It's his embarrassment, not ours. Mr. Rachett was the name he gave. Mr. Rachett. Perhaps you know him."

Dupin shook his head.

"We would be happy to let you try the coat on," the salesman suggested.

"I don't think I'm interested," Dupin said. "Though I am getting married and shall want a better coat soon."

"May I offer my congratulations, sir," the salesman intoned with a bow.

* * *

Edmund kept running between his room and the café. One moment he was sure Mr. Dupin had deserted him, the next, that Mr. Dupin was late only because he'd discovered word of Sis and had gone to fetch her. Then, not knowing what to think, he spent the time inventing new calamities.

Another hour passed before Edmund saw Dupin. He was coming down Wickenden Street, not in a hurry, merely strolling, gazing now this way, now that.

Edmund, close to tears, rushed up to him.

Dupin stopped, studied the boy, frowned and said, "What is the matter now?"

Edmund stared at him in disbelief. "You said you'd wait for me at the café."

"Do you think I have nothing better to do with my time than sit about in such places?"

"But . . ."

"Edmund," Dupin announced, "I could use a drink." He started for the café.

Edmund stood his ground.

Dupin looked back over his shoulder. "I have received news of your sister," he said and continued on.

Edmund's resolution dropped away. He raced to catch up.

10

THE ONE WHO MURDERED HER

DUPIN TOOK THE table where they had sat that morning, then ordered whiskey for himself.

"Are you hungry?" he asked Edmund.

Unable to think of anything but what Mr. Dupin might tell him, the boy shook his head.

Dupin dismissed the waiter. To Edmund he said, "Stop making yourself look so miserable."

Suddenly, the thought came to Edmund that Mr. Dupin had learned something terrible but was only waiting before announcing it. He shrank back in his seat.

Paying no mind to the boy, Dupin drank for a while, then abruptly asked, "What have you been doing with yourself?"

Edmund looked at him with surprise, "You gave me a message to deliver to Mrs. Whitman," he answered.

"Did I?"

It was impossible for Edmund to reply.

"Did I?" Dupin repeated.

"Yes, sir."

Dupin leaned over the table and said softly, "Did you see her?"

"Mr. Dupin, you told me to."

"Was she very beautiful?"

"Yes, sir."

"And did you give her the message as I instructed, only to her and when she was alone?"

Edmund nodded.

"How did she look when she received it?"

"Mr. Dupin, you said you had found . . ."

Dupin held up a hand to cut him short. "Never mind. I can imagine it." He closed his eyes.

"Mrs. Whitman asked me to give you a message."

Dupin looked up eagerly. "Which was?"

"That you were to come, not at four o'clock, but at three-thirty. To the cemetery on Church Street, behind the house, so you can meet privately. No one goes there, she said."

"Good!" Dupin exclaimed and drank again.

"Mr. Dupin, you told me that you've found something about my sister. Is that true?"

Dupin looked up from his drink. "Who?"

"My sister," Edmund whispered.

"Ah, yes. Your sister. Yes, I found out something."

Edmund sat bolt upright. "What?" he got out.

"I know why she was stolen."

"Why?"

"I'm not prepared to divulge that —"

"But . . . !"

"— so you need not ask me anymore."

"Mr. Dupin. . . . !"

"Nothing!"

Deeply frustrated, Edmund watched Dupin, trying to understand him. He remembered the questions Mrs. Whitman had asked about the man. He thought of the least offensive one, screwed up his courage, and said, "Mr. Dupin?"

"What?"

"Where is your home?"

Dupin glowered. "Why do you ask?"

"Mrs. Whitman was surprised you were here."

"She needn't have been."

"Are you here . . . on business?"

"In a manner of speaking."

"Can I ask . . . what . . . business?"

"No."

Stymied, Edmund cast about for another approach. But before he could think of what to try next, Dupin abruptly reached across the table, touched his arm, and said, "Mrs. Whitman is a remarkable woman, isn't she?"

Edmund didn't know how to answer.

"Helen," Dupin boldly proclaimed, placing fingers to his heart, "I love now — now for the first and only time." Once more he leaned over the table and in a voice full of solicitude, said, "Do you think I should marry her?"

It was the second time that day an adult had asked Edmund's advice. "I don't know, sir," he stammered.

"Edmund, I wish you would tell me — in your own words — how Mrs. Whitman received my letter."

Edmund's eyes began to fill with tears.

Dupin scowled. "Now what?"

"Please tell me what's happened to Sis."

"No."

"I thought you had gone too," Edmund continued, his voice choked, "that I wouldn't see you again. You even left your notebook."

"And you read it."

Edmund shook his head.

Dupin smiled thinly. "Edmund, you asked me my business. I shall tell you a great truth. Are you listening?"

"Yes, sir."

"I am a creator of the future."

"The future? Whose?"

"Mine. And yours."

"What about Sis?"

"Hers as well."

"Can you tell me . . . what will happen to her?"

Dupin looked at the boy curiously. "You read my notes. I am working on that."

Edmund blushed but asked finally, "Is she alive?"

"People say I love death. Do you think so? Well, what difference does it make what you think? It takes us all. You don't trust me, do you?"

It was too much. Edmund leaned over the table and pressed his face in his arms.

Dupin's eyes flashed with anger. "Edmund, do not take my kindness for granted. I'm very close to bringing this business to a satisfactory conclusion, but one rude word from you and I shall drop it entirely."

Edmund tried to stifle his tears.

Dupin leaned across to him. "Soon," he said soothingly, "soon we shall have a solution. But it shall be *my* solution in *my* time.

"Now," he declared, "I need to shave and change. Can you fetch water to your room?"

"Yes, sir," Edmund mumbled.

"Then lead the way."

Only as they were walking did Edmund remember what had happened in his room. "Sir," he said, "when I came back from Mrs. Whitman's, and you weren't at the café, I thought you might have gone to the room, so I went there."

Dupin shrugged.

Edmund said, "Someone else had been there."

Dupin stopped. "What do you mean?"

"The room was torn up. Someone had opened Aunty's trunk."

"Why didn't you tell me before?" Dupin demanded angrily.

"I forgot."

"Forgot!" Dupin cried. "You are the dullest of boys! If I don't resolve this business it shall be your fault."

Edmund felt as if he'd been struck.

"Now, quickly, lead me there!"

As they hurried now, Dupin asked, "What was taken?"

"At first I thought nothing," Edmund managed to say. "Then I realized a picture was taken."

"A picture?"

"From Aunty's trunk. It was of my mum and Aunty. Made just before Mum left for America."

Dupin stopped again and looked hard at Edmund. Then he said, "Is there anything else you have forgotten to inform me about?"

Edmund struggled to keep from blurting out his frustration. "No, sir. I don't think so."

Dupin kept staring. Then he said, "Edmund, you are lying." And he turned on his heel and began to walk fast again.

Edmund hurried after him but for the rest of the way neither spoke.

At the room Dupin took one look at the trunk and said, "It wasn't forced."

Edmund looked at him blankly.

"The person who opened it had a key," Dupin explained.

"Only my aunty had one," Edmund said.

"Then the person who came here took it from her. No doubt the person who murdered her." Dupin stood up.

Edmund felt his heart contract. "*Was* she . . . murdered then?"

"Of course."

"But *why*?" Edmund cried.

"Edmund, I am soon due at Mrs. Whitman's." Dupin held out the basin. "I require water to wash."

With a sudden movement, Edmund struck it aside. It clattered to the floor. Dupin jumped back. For a moment the two stared at one another. Then Dupin turned away. "Please be quick about it."

Sullenly, Edmund retrieved the basin and left the room. By the time he returned Dupin had changed his shirt. Now he proceeded to shave.

Edmund sat on his bed and watched. One moment he wanted to scream out his rage at Mr. Dupin. The next he thought he should get on his knees and beg him to show some mercy. Then he thought the wisest thing of all would be to run away. But in the end all he said was, "Shall I go with you to Mrs. Whitman's?"

Dupin stopped brushing his jacket, "Under no circumstances," he snapped.

After a moment, Edmund said, "Then what should I do?"

"Anything you wish."

"Should I wait here?"

"I suppose."

"When will you get back?"

"Edmund, it doesn't matter to me where the devil you are. Just not Mrs. Whitman's." He slipped into his coat.

Edmund pulled the blanket around himself. "I'll stay here."

Dupin approached the door.

Feeling a rising desperation Edmund cast about for some way to hold him. "Mr. Dupin," he suddenly said, "there *is* something I haven't told you."

Dupin opened the door. "Is there?" he said, the sarcasm in his voice making the boy wince.

"It's about my father," Edmund said.

Dupin froze. "What about him?"

"I told you he had been lost at sea," Edmund began slowly, finding it difficult to talk through the tightness he felt in his throat. "That's what Aunty told us to say. It's true. But . . . that was my *first* father who died. My mother remarried. It was my . . . stepfather who . . ."

Dupin became very pale. He turned at the door. "Stepfather!" he gasped. "Have you a stepfather too?"

The depth of Dupin's reaction frightened Edmund. He shrank back. "Yes, sir," he whispered. "I do."

"And you never told me . . ."

"Aunty said I mustn't," Edmund pleaded, close to tears. "I'm only trying to do what she says. He abandoned Mum. After taking her money. It was right after they married."

"His name?"

Edmund gulped back his tears and said, "I think . . . I never met him . . . it was a . . . Mr. Rachett."

"Rachett!" Dupin exclaimed, stepping further back into the room.

"I can't remember," Edmund wailed in agony. "He misled her and abandoned her. I don't even know what he looks like."

Dupin stood over Edmund. "But would he know *you*?"

"Mr. Dupin," Edmund cried miserably, "I don't know anything!"

"But I know," Dupin shouted. "Because he *did* see you!"

Shocked, Edmund looked up. "What do you mean? When? Where? How do you know?"

"This morning you went in search of a coat, did you not? You entered a clothing store and were chased out. When you were there a Mr. Rachett saw you, and fled."

"Are you sure?" Edmund stammered.

"Edmund, will you never learn. I am *always* sure!" He leaned close to the boy. "The question is this: can you, who were in the same place with him, can *you* describe *him*?"

Edmund thought desperately. "Mr. Dupin, he was standing on a box. He seemed big. And fat. Whiskers, I think . . ." He shook his head. "That's all," he admitted. Then he said, "Did he kill Aunty?"

"Edmund, are there more details you've been keeping from me?"

Edmund felt his face grow red. But giving way to emotional exhaustion, he nodded. "It's about . . . about why my mum was coming to America."

"So when I asked you about that this morning and you said you didn't know, you lied."

"Mr. Dupin," Edmund cried, "Aunty said . . . I have no one to help me. I need . . ."

"Out with it!" Dupin barked.

Edmund pushed himself into a corner and gulped down

his pain. Finally he said, "My mum wanted to find my . . . this . . . Mr. Rachett to get back our money and" — his voice sank into a whisper — "divorce him. It's not done in England. It had to be done here. In America."

"*Did* she find him?"

"I don't know, sir. Truly," Edmund begged. "Please. Aunty said I must never tell. That's why I didn't. Please. You must believe me."

Dupin stared down at Edmund. "Do you know how much alike you and I are?"

"What?"

"So much the same — even to the stepfather. Except . . ." Dupin added, "except for one thing." His eyes were full of torment.

"What is it?" Edmund asked.

"The death," Dupin replied somberly, "of Sis."

"Don't say that!" Edmund shouted. "You mustn't. She's not dead. She isn't!"

Dupin continued to stare at the boy.

Edmund flung himself down and buried his face on the bed.

Dupin went to the door. There he paused. "Edmund . . ." he said softly.

Edmund could not face the man. He wished desperately for a word of kindness.

"You said you were familiar with the workers on the docks. Is that true?"

"Yes . . ."

"Anyone who can tell you about current ships?"

"Captain Elias."

"Find this Captain Elias and inquire if there's a ship called *The Lady Liberty*. Where she hails from. Date of arrival. Cargo. In particular, the names of her watchmen."

Edmund forced himself to sit up. "Can't you tell me why?"

"I wish to know if a Mr. Fortnoy lied under oath," Dupin said.

"Mr. Fortnoy?"

"He was there on the dock last night. The white-haired one. Do you recall?"

Edmund thought hard. Remembering, he nodded.

"He's the one I believe murdered your aunt." So saying, Dupin departed.

PART TWO

11

BEYOND THE CEMETERY GATE

AN EXHAUSTED EDMUND remained on the bed staring after Dupin. One moment he was convinced that everything the man said was true. The next he was just as certain it was all mad, the product of drink. The only thing Edmund knew for sure was that *he* himself didn't know what to think. It was impossible to settle on anything!

With a violent shake of his head he came to a decision: he could no longer bear the agony of confusion. He would put Mr. Dupin to a test. If he went to Mrs. Whitman as he said he was going to do, Edmund would stay with him. But if Mr. Dupin did not go to the graveyard, if he had lied, he would leave him. He would seek help elsewhere. With a new sense of urgency Edmund rushed down the steps and onto the street.

Though fog and drizzle had turned the day even gloomier, Mr. Dupin was not that hard to spot. The long black coat he wore, his slow, plodding walk, allowed Edmund to follow without himself being seen.

But a few blocks beyond Wickenden, on Benefit Street, Edmund began to wonder if he was the only one following the man. Someone else was walking between him and Dupin. Whenever Dupin stopped — which he did a number of times — this person stopped as well.

Edmund, wanting to know who it was, quickened his step. But as he drew closer the same fog which had afforded him protection from discovery made it difficult to see who the stranger was. Then, just when he was near enough to see, the figure vanished.

Mystified, Edmund recalled his notion of the night before, that a ghost had been hovering near when he came out of his building. But once again he could almost hear his aunty saying, *"Edmund! There are no such things as ghosts."* So when he saw nothing more, not even a shadow, he decided he'd only imagined some stranger.

A little beyond the Unitarian Church, Dupin abruptly halted. As far as Edmund could tell, he appeared to be gazing at the back of some large brick buildings which abutted the hill below. Then he turned and looked at the church, studying the fog-shrouded steeple. Dupin pulled out his watch and after consulting it, took hasty strides back to the church. To Edmund's dismay, he entered.

Mr. Dupin had failed the test. He was not going to Mrs. Whitman's.

Deeply disappointed, the boy retreated into a doorway across the street. There, eyes on the church entrance, he waited mournfully, hoping against hope that he was wrong about Mr. Dupin. But he began thinking about where else he could go, to whom else he might turn.

*   *   *

It was dim inside the church. By the light of a few candles set in sconces, Dupin scrutinized its vast space looking for steps to the steeple. What he saw were rows of pews and lines of prayer books tucked in front railings. The words *First Unitarian Church* stamped upon them ran from pew to pew like a glimmering thread of gold.

Halfway up the empty aisle Dupin paused, sensing that all about him there were people huddled. His heart began beating rapidly. Were these people alive or dead? Unable to find the steeple steps he retreated anxiously. It was then that he discovered, to the left of the entrance, the very steps he wanted. He started up.

Dupin climbed until he reached the bell room where the dangling ropes hung in rows. The height made him feel giddy. Alarmed, he grasped one of the ropes for support. The feel of it reminded him of something. Thoughtfully, he stroked the rope with his fingertips, then drew the string he'd found in the bank vault from his pocket. He compared it with the bell rope. It was the same substance, hemp.

Dupin put the string away, and gazed through the steeple window down onto Benefit Street. Though the thin rain and growing darkness obscured his view, he was able to make out the same row of buildings he had studied from below. But what he saw now was a narrow, cobblestone alley, all but hidden, which ran from Benefit halfway down College Hill. There, against a building, it came to an end. That building — he recognized it from the shape of its singular roof — was the Providence Bank.

It would be easy, Dupin saw, for a horse and carriage to go down that alley and so come directly against the rear of the bank. Moreover, if one stood atop the carriage it would be just as easy to climb onto the bank's roof.

Dupin scanned the roof with meticulous care, searching for the opening of the air shaft which he knew rose from the vault. There, he saw it. *No grown person could go down that narrow shaft.*

Ah, thought Dupin, but a *child* — just the idea of it made Dupin shudder — a child could be lowered down. That child could then have loaded gold, brick by brick, into a basket which would be hauled away. Then that same child could have been pulled up too. Nothing would be left.

And yet — Dupin reminded himself — two things *had* been left. A button. And . . . Dupin's fingers reached for the string. Not *string*, he told himself, but a bit of *rope*, rope uscd to lower the child down the shaft which was so much like a deep and narrow grave. Dupin shuddered again.

* * *

When Dupin reappeared on the street, Edmund was enormously relieved. But the closer Dupin drew to Mrs.

Whitman's house, the more slowly he walked. Edmund hung back. Sometimes Dupin stopped completely as if not sure whether to proceed. Once he did an about-face and started retracing his steps. That sent Edmund scurrying. The next moment, however, showing more determination than ever, the man strode purposefully to Mrs. Whitman's. And once there, he passed down Church Street. Mr. Dupin had done, after all, what he said he would do.

Edmund let out a sigh. He felt so much better, in fact, that he made up his mind to go after the information Mr. Dupin wanted about *The Lady Liberty.*

But no sooner did he start to turn than the front door of Mrs. Whitman's house opened. Out burst Catherine, the maid, a coat held about her head and shoulders. And she didn't walk, but rather ran up the street.

Watching her, Edmund remembered her hostility. He didn't know the reason for it but hadn't Mrs. Whitman herself warned him? Now, just as Mrs. Whitman was about to meet Mr. Dupin, Catherine was rushing from the house. Edmund felt it would be a good notion to see where she was going.

Catherine hurried up the steep incline of the street called Jenkes. At the corner she turned and moved along Congdon Street. Then, just before Meeting Street, she darted into a large building.

Curious, but cautious, Edmund studied the sign over its door.

*   *   *

Dupin stood before the rusty iron gate to the small ceme-tery. The old burial ground — crowded with gravestones and even a small mausoleum — had been cut from the side of the hill in the space between Mrs. Whitman's house and the rear of a church. A large willow tree, trailing leafless branches, dripped tears of rain like a professional mourner on ground already soggy underfoot. Untrimmed bramble hedges rose on all sides, creating a compressed wilderness.

Through the clinging mist Dupin examined the rear of the house. He wondered if Edmund had understood the message right, that he was to meet her in such a place. Not that he was displeased with the notion. He rather liked it. To speak of love amidst death and decay seemed correct, even proper for him. It fit his mood. His facts. His life.

But should he or should he not propose to her?

Dupin reminded himself that a marriage was a good idea, a necessary one. Normality. Stability. Money. Once again he vowed to move forward with the plan. Still, he wished he had a drink.

Hands trembling, Dupin pushed the cemetery gate open. His boots squashed into the soft ground and made him wonder on whose bones he trod.

He approached the mausoleum. It was no more than five feet in height, with columns around its central door, and looked like an ancient Roman temple.

Dupin decided that if he stood at the mausoleum entrance

it would create the impression that he was just emerging from it. The image — *emerging from death* – pleased him enormously. The perfect place for Mrs. Whitman to find him. Wasn't that exactly what his love was?

Dupin took another step toward the tomb. He stopped, astonished. The temple door was opening, a figure emerging. It was a woman. Her dress was dark, her hair long and fair, her face chalky white, ghost-like.

Heart hammering, Dupin called, "Helen? Is that you?"

The woman stood motionless. She seemed to be staring right at him. Into him.

Dupin took another step forward. Suddenly he realized that it was not Mrs. Whitman but someone all his senses insisted was a person he had only recently seen.

"My children," the figure whispered hoarsely.

Dupin's blood ran cold.

"Where are my children!"

With a gasp, Dupin realized who was standing before him: the woman taken from the bay. *The murdered woman.*

"What have you done with my children!" the woman cried again. She was creeping toward Dupin, reaching at him with long, pale fingers.

"I don't have them," Dupin stammered, too horrified to move. "I don't!"

"Give them to me!" the woman pleaded, still advancing. Abruptly she stopped. Her eyes grew wide with terror. She seemed to be looking through Dupin, beyond him. With a scream she turned and fled into the fog and brambles.

Dupin flung himself in the opposite direction, tripping over a fallen gravestone. Regaining his balance, he plunged forward wildly, only to be grasped by huge, powerful hands.

"Help!" Dupin screamed. *"Help!"* Frantically, he twisted about to see who held him. It was Throck.

12

TO SEE A GHOST

EDMUND WAS STILL standing behind a hedge, the entrance of the Hotel American House, when Catherine came rushing out. This time a man was with her. Against the weather he wore a tall hat and a muffler which all but hid his great spread of whiskers. As Edmund looked on, the two hurried off the same way Catherine had come. Edmund tagged behind, keeping his distance.

Suddenly, he realized who the man was. It was the one he'd seen trying on a coat at the clothier that morning, the very one Mr. Dupin claimed was Mr. Rachett, his stepfather! Astounded, Edmund stopped short, then came back to his senses just in time to see the two enter Mrs. Whitman's house.

Panting for breath, Edmund stood before the closed door trying to decide what action to take. He could steal back behind the house where, he assumed, Mr. Dupin was meeting Mrs. Whitman and tell Mr. Dupin about Mr. Rachett. Then he remembered the man's words, that he must keep away. The last thing Edmund wanted to do was antagonize him again. No, news of Mr. Rachett would have to wait while he went in search of information about *The Lady Liberty*. Resolved, Edmund started off for the docks.

But so preoccupied was the boy with thoughts of Mr. Rachett he never noticed that since he'd turned his back on the Hotel American House, he himself was being followed.

*　　*　　*

"Let me go!" Dupin gasped, trying to wrench free from Throck's iron grip.

"Here now," the night watchman returned. "It's you who ran into me!" All the same he took his hands from Dupin's shoulders.

Set free, Dupin instantly swung about, gazing with terrified eyes through the brambles and fog at the mausoleum. Whatever it was that he had seen had vanished. "Did you see anything?" he demanded of Throck.

"What are you talking about?" the night watchman growled suspiciously.

"There!" cried Dupin, pointing where he had seen the figure. "The ghost of a woman. Standing before the mausoleum. Demanding her children."

"I don't see a thing."

"There was!"

"You're daft."

Dupin, legs shaking, walked back toward the mausoleum

but stopped when he saw that its door was still open. He made a nervous half turn toward Throck. The night watchman stood a few feet behind, peering at Dupin with intense puzzlement.

Dupin pushed himself forward again, edging closer to the tomb. "Is someone there?" he called nervously.

All he heard was his own labored breathing and the monotonous dripping of the rain.

Fighting against the terror he felt, Dupin climbed the steps to the mausoleum and placed his hand on the door. The cold iron drove a spike of chill through him. Summoning what strength remained to him, he grasped the door handle and pulled.

With a rasping, grating sound the door opened further. Dupin, leaning forward, attempted to look into the dark. The stench of decay brought a wave of nausea. It forced him to back out.

Sweating profusely, he clung to the door frame and leaned forward. "Hello!" he called in a hoarse whisper. Only an echo answered.

Gradually, his eyes grew accustomed to the dark. There on the floor he saw — long and narrow — what appeared to be a body.

With a hammering heart, Dupin crept inside the mausoleum. As he did so his eyes remained fixed upon the form on the floor. Tentatively, he put his foot forward. There was a soft, crinkling sound. Steeling himself, he touched the object with shaking fingers. It was a straw mattress.

As he bent to examine it, Dupin sensed that someone was in the doorway. With a start, he stood up and turned. Throck had followed him into the mausoleum.

Dupin recalled the man as he'd first seen him at the docks, hovering over the dead woman. A feeling of dread engulfed him. "What are you doing here?" he demanded.

"You're the odd one to be asking that," Throck retorted dryly.

"What do you mean?" Dupin said.

Throck, his mouth fixed in a leer, took a step forward, his powerful form completely blocking the way. "I seen you in court this morning," he said. "You were spying on me, weren't you?"

"No, not at all."

"Two can play this game, can't they?" Throck continued. "Well, this time, I followed you. Not that you knew it. And where do you go? Right to the Providence Bank. Where that robbery took place, wasn't it? How's that for detail?

"Then off you go back down to Fox Point to be with that boy? That boy. Always that boy. Makes a man wonder. Makes *me* wonder. Are you his father? I says to myself. Then you come back — trailing that boy — and stop to take a gander at the back of that same bank. So, never mind what *I'm* doing here. What I'm asking you is this. What are *you* doing in this abandoned graveyard where no one ever comes?"

Dupin attempted to draw himself up. "I am here . . . to meet someone," he replied.

"Far as I can see," Throck sneered, "you and me, we're

alone. Saving the dead, of course, but then, they won't help you none. Not now."

"I don't care what you see," Dupin cried. "I'm telling the truth!"

"And what," Throck said, coming further into the crypt, "what if I happen not to believe you?"

Dupin looked for a way past him. As he did a figure loomed up behind the night watchman. The woman again.

"*There!*" Dupin screamed, pointing and shrinking back. "*There!*"

Throck spun around.

"Is that you, Mr. Poe?" Mrs. Whitman asked.

Pushing by Throck, Dupin stepped out of the mausoleum. Mrs. Whitman stood at the foot of the steps, gazing up, shawl over her shoulders to protect herself from the drizzle. For a moment she and Dupin simply looked at each other.

Then Dupin, struggling to pull himself together, turned to Throck. "You see," he said in a voice not altogether firm, "there *is* a woman."

Throck scrutinized Mrs. Whitman. "Is this man," he asked, "some friend of yours?"

"He is," she replied.

"And were you to meet him here?"

"I was. Is something the matter?" she asked.

"No, nothing," Dupin quickly answered. "I think you may go," he said to Throck.

Throck began to speak, but saw Mrs. Whitman's stern eyes upon him and changed his mind. Sullenly, he walked to the gate and out to the street. There he turned and leveled a finger at Dupin. "Don't you forget. I'll be watching," he called. "Throck sees it through."

Dupin kept his eyes upon Throck until the night watchman lumbered out of sight. Then, leaning against the mausoleum door, he tried to calm himself.

Mrs. Whitman watched him anxiously. "Mr. Poe," she said, "what is happening? Why are you looking so ghastly? Who was that dreadful man? Why was he here? No one ever comes here."

"I can't explain," Dupin replied weakly.

"You look as if you had seen a ghost."

Dupin started. "I have."

Mrs. Whitman stood a little straighter. "Mr. Poe," she demanded in a shocked but urgent whisper, "have you been drinking?"

Dupin shook his head.

"Then what is it?"

"I'm in dreadful pain," he said, reaching out. "Great pain. Please, give me your hand."

"Mr. Poe . . ."

"I have been so alone, so . . ."

"Mr. Poe. It's not wise for us to remain here. My mother has invited people for tea. They are gathering in the parlor at this very minute."

"Just a few moments," Dupin begged. He was not sure he

could walk even the short distance to the house. "Helen, my life has been miserable without you."

Mrs. Whitman took a step toward him, but stopped herself and glanced back over her shoulder. "Please," she insisted. "We cannot remain here. I can't have scandal."

Dupin sighed, closed his eyes and again held out a hand. "There is so much I need to tell you."

Mrs. Whitman began to reach toward him.

"I sent you a note last night," he said.

Her hand halted. "I never received it," she said.

Dupin opened his eyes.

"My mother intercepted it," Mrs. Whitman explained. "But you mustn't say anything about it. Now, please, Mr. Poe, take possession of yourself, and come with me into the house. And be warned: We will be surrounded by enemies." So saying, she forced herself to turn about and walk up the path toward the rear door of the house.

Dupin, pausing only to look wonderingly back at the mausoleum, followed.

13

OUR SECRET FEARS

"WILL YOU BE all right?" Mrs. Whitman asked the moment they were inside.

Dupin pressed trembling hands over his face, then withdrew them. "Helen, I love as I've never loved . . ."

"I beg you," she whispered urgently. "Not now. I will be missed. Follow me."

Dupin held her back. "You said they were enemies. I'm not sure I can. You don't know how weak I am."

"You must. They are testing us and we are expected." She reached up and gently touched his face. "Come," she said softly. "If you believe in me. And us."

Sweating, almost overwhelmed by tension, Dupin followed her into the parlor. Five people were there, all dressed in black. All had teacups in their hands. All were talking genially. But when Dupin entered, conversation ceased.

"May I present," Mrs. Whitman announced, "Mr. Edgar Allan Poe."

Dupin made a slight bow but as he did a shock went through him. Every one of the women he saw had the face of the apparition in the tomb. Every man resembled Edmund. Yet even as he gazed at them, they shifted and blurred into a single death's-head. Then one by one they changed again, each becoming some distinct spectral figure.

Dupin knew then where he had come: He had descended into a gathering of demons, a masque of black death.

"Mr. Poe," Dupin heard Mrs. Whitman say as if at a great distance, "here is my mother, Mrs. Powers." She indicated an elderly woman who from her chair acknowledged Dupin with a curt nod. Dupin saw only her arm, the same ghost-like arm he had seen taking his letter at the door the night before.

"This is Dr. Dillard," Mrs. Whitman continued, turning toward a plump man with very pink cheeks. He wore a clerical collar. "His orations at funerals are famous here in Providence."

"How do you do, sir," Dr. Dillard said, his lips pressed into a tight smile.

Dupin noted only a hideous, satanic grin.

"And Mrs. Dillard," Mrs. Whitman went on, referring to a tiny woman who sat by the minister's side. She offered a nervous smile in Dupin's direction.

In her, Dupin saw Death's consort.

"And here is Mr. Arnold," Mrs. Whitman said.

When Dupin looked at the whiskered man he saw nothing but a figure gross with greed and lust.

"A great pleasure to meet the celebrated Mr. Poe," Arnold intoned boldly. "Mr. Poe of 'The Raven,' and 'The Gold Bug.' I am, sir, your literary admirer. You have informed me much about the darker passions."

Dupin managed a stiff smile. "Thank you, sir," he said.

"And finally," Mrs. Whitman concluded, "Mr. McFarlane. Mr. McFarlane is one of our own Providence poets."

"But not so fortunate in glory or genius as the famous Mr. Poe," said McFarlane, a bald, cheerful-looking man. Dupin took him for a devil.

Introductions over, Dupin felt them all staring at him with venomous eyes.

"Catherine," Mrs. Whitman called anxiously. "Some tea for Mr. Poe."

Arnold approached Dupin, offered his hand, and said, "I have long wanted to meet you, sir."

Dupin turned, wondering what torture this monstrous creature had prepared for him.

"I have read much of your work," Arnold continued, his voice growing loud as he warmed to his inquiry, "and I have always wondered how you came up with your ideas. That is to say, Mr. Poe, your tales have the most fantastical notions. All these stories of crime, brutality, death . . ." Arnold shifted about to catch Mrs. Powers's eye. "Do these things," he said, turning back to Dupin, "come from within *you*, sir? Why so much concern with *evil*?"

Dupin was reminded of the fright he'd just experienced in the cemetery, and wondered what this beast might have to do with it.

"Or perhaps," Arnold pressed when Dupin did not answer, "the question upsets you?"

"No," Dupin forced himself to say. "Not so."

"Please," Arnold urged. "I wish you would explain."

Trying to steady himself, Dupin passed a hand over his face. Suddenly he understood who these monsters were: They were his own creations, his own torments, his own pain. Confront them, he said to himself. Tell them what they are and they will go.

"Evil," he began . . . but faltered. "Evil is only the name we give . . . our secret fears."

"Fears?" Dr. Dillard demanded from across the room. "Of what?"

"The fears . . . in our hearts," Dupin continued, trying to untangle his thoughts, and speaking barely above a whisper.

"Ah!" Arnold cried, "as in your 'Tell-Tale Heart,' and 'The Gold Bug'?"

" 'The Tell-Tale Heart.' "

"I must protest," Dr. Dillard declared. "I, for one, have no such fears within me."

"Quite right, Dr. Dillard," McFarlane was quick to add.

"Nor do I. As for the ladies, certainly *they* have no such fears." He made a bow toward Mrs. Whitman.

"Could you give us more of an explanation?" Dr. Dillard asked.

Dupin pressed his hands together tightly, tried to smile, but failed. "What I believe," he said finally, his voice strained, "is that writers write about what they know best. And," he concluded, "what some writers know best is what they fear."

"Could you," McFarlane said, "give us an example?" There was a trace of mockery in his voice.

Dupin, aware that he was being put to a crucial test, felt a renewed onslaught of nervousness. His eyes swept around his tormentors.

"Anything?" Arnold insisted from across the room.

Dupin found himself floundering again. With a look he appealed to Mrs. Whitman.

"Perhaps," she prompted, "from *ordinary* life."

It was the help Dupin needed. He remembered something. "Yes," he announced, "I can give you an example. A puzzle." He studied the grotesque faces before him. "A puzzle which, if we could fully understand it would bring . . . truth."

"Do say," urged Mrs. Powers.

"If a man," Dupin began, "if a man orders a coat, a fine coat, has it made and fitted, and yet, at the last moment chooses *not* to take it, might . . . might not the reason why he decides thus yield some important facts, so that what appears to be irrational becomes rational?"

"What has this to do with fear?" Mrs. Powers exclaimed. "Why, Mr. Arnold, where are you going?"

Dupin, startled, swung about. Mr. Arnold, red-faced and flustered, was standing by the door. "My apologies. I must go!" he announced.

"But, Mr. Arnold . . ." Mrs. Powers called.

"Urgent business," he murmured and bowed himself out.

Dupin stared after him trying to make sense of what had just happened. He decided he had smitten one of his enemies. He felt his tension ease.

While the other guests chatted quietly amongst themselves, Dupin carefully sipped his tea and tried to calm his nerves. The creatures in the room were beginning to look more like people. To his left sat Mrs. Whitman. Mr. McFarlane was on his right.

"I should think," Mrs. Whitman said to McFarlane, "that Mr. Poe's poem 'The Raven' is the most profound poetic expression America has ever produced."

"Oh, yes," McFarlane agreed, "we can all readily agree to that. But it just seems so . . . What shall I say, Mr. Poe? . . . so different from your tales, sir."

"How are my tales different?"

"I must admit," McFarlane said, "they make me feel very uncomfortable. Almost unclean. There is something of the sublime in 'Nevermore . . .' But then we have 'The Murders in the Rue Morgue,' with this character you invented, this Auguste Dupin. I must say he's a most improbable personage."

"What are your objections?" Dupin asked.

"Why, sir, to speak with honesty, no man could reason as your Dupin does. Besides, I felt the story to be a low, bestial, sordid thing. It appalled me. And, sir, I mean you no offence but I see none of *that* sordidness on your face."

Mrs. Whitman attempted to laugh lightly. "Come now, Mr. McFarlane," she said, "can you read so much from a face?"

McFarlane smiled. "I for one believe in the reading of faces. Don't you, Mr. Poe?"

Dupin, no longer feeling himself under attack, turned to Mrs. Whitman and gazed calmly at her. He even smiled, then looked about the room. There were only people now. He had won. "Every fear, every image," he said as much to himself as to the others, "has two sides."

"I quite agree," McFarlane interjected. "Good things seem to be readily apparent. But the bad —"

Again Dupin addressed Mrs. Whitman. "What can you read from my face?" he asked.

Mrs. Whitman blushed. "I should need more time," she managed to say.

"As much as you need," Dupin returned gallantly.

"Did you know," she informed him with a nervous laugh, "an establishment for the making of daguerreotypes has opened in the city."

"Ah, yes," McFarlane interjected. "In the Arcade. I have heard they make fine images."

"Now, Mr. Poe," Mrs. Whitman went on, "if you were to have a portrait made and I had it in my possession, I might be able to study your character at my leisure."

"Where are you staying, Mr. Poe?" Mrs. Powers suddenly interjected.

"With some friends," he replied.

"With anyone we might know?"

"I don't believe so."

"And how long shall you be staying?"

"That depends."

"On what?"

"On Mrs. Whitman."

Mrs. Whitman blushed again.

Dupin set aside his tea cup and stood. "I am going directly to that daguerreotype studio," he announced. "I shall see what kind of an image they can produce and I shall offer it to you, so you may study it at your leisure."

"But Mr. Poe," Mrs. Powers snapped, "which image of yourself shall you present?"

"I never know," Dupin returned.

14

OVER THE EDGE

"IT'S MASTER EDMUND!" Captain Elias cried when Edmund approached him on the quay. "You've been keeping yourself away. Did that sparkling sister of yours turn up right enough?"

In the short while Edmund had been in Providence he'd spent enough time at the docks — in the company of his sister — to have made friends with some of the regular workmen. In particular he'd become close to a dock hand he knew as Captain Elias.

The man had spent most of his life at sea. Now old, he'd been given a job of weighing out small cargoes on the wharves. Even Edmund suspected that the rank "Captain" was one he'd given himself, but he seemed to know everything about the port of Providence. In exchange for their meager news — their dull days, his sister's complaints about Aunty Pru — to which the captain had listened with considerable sympathy, he had been more than willing to share his mind and experience.

But as glad as Edmund was to see his friend, he had no heart to explain about his sister. It was information he wanted. "She's home," he said.

"Well then," the captain returned, "it's not much good for anyone to be out today. And your proper aunty?" he inquired.

"Home too," Edmund said, feeling obliged to spin out the lie.

"Do you know," the captain said, dropping a wink even as he set a tea chest on his scales. "I thought I saw your aunty."

"Did you!" Edmund cried. "When?"

The captain grinned at the boy's reaction. "I said I only *thought* so, lad. Mind, you've never brought the lady 'round so I've not had the pleasure of her acquaintance, have I?"

Edmund shook his head.

"But I'll tell you. This morning, early as can be, a lady rather like what you've described was wandering about. Half distracted she was, her clothing in terrible tatters."

"It wasn't my aunt."

"Oh, I realized that soon enough," agreed the Captain. "For like I said, Master Edmund, this one only reminded me of your description in a kind of interesting way. As for this unfortunate lady she was asking about the dead woman."

"The one found in the bay last night?"

"It's all the talk here. A ghastly thing. There was to be an

131

inquest today which is what I told this lady. She was that interested. Distracted ones get drawn to such things, you see."

"Who was she?"

"So I asked myself, Master Edmund, not that I have a start to knowing. But I can see by your eyes you take such things to heart too. Well you might. Every death is a mortal warning. Mind, I never saw the dead woman myself though I had my part in it."

"What do you mean?"

"See, it was Fortnoy who found her."

"Mr. Fortnoy?" Edmund said, remembering what Mr. Dupin had said about the man.

"Himself. He's a good friend of mine."

Edmund backed up a step. "He is?"

"To be sure," the captain returned. "It was when Fortnoy was rowing back from his watch that he found her. That's where I came in. It was me who relieved Fortnoy so he could come ashore."

Edmund's heart seemed to stand still. "Do you know where he had been?"

"Like I said, lad, on his ship."

"I don't understand."

"You see his ship was —"

"*The Lady Liberty!*" Edmund blurted out.

"Ah, you know her! She's an old ship. A Nova Scotia brig out of Halifax. Captain Davis her master. And a hard driver, that one. It was he who made Fortnoy stand watch three days running without a break." Elias shook his head. "Can you imagine. Locked up, so to speak, for three days."

"Three days?" said Edmund weakly. If that were true perhaps Mr. Dupin was wrong about the man. . . .

"Three days," said Captain Elias emphatically. "Not once was he let off till I went to relieve him."

"Captain Elias, are you very sure?"

"I've not the slightest doubt. These things have a way of getting known. No one will stand watch on her now. Not for love nor money."

"Is she in port?"

"Sure she is. And this Davis has got to do the watch himself. Now, Master Edmund, if you've time to hear a good yarn, I've one for you. You see, *The Lady Liberty* had a sister ship. *Seahawk*, her name was —"

"Captain Elias, are you so very sure your friend was on *The Lady Liberty* for *three* days?"

"Master Edmund, I'm as sure as I'm sitting here and talking to you. Did you want to hear that other yarn?"

"I don't have time now."

"Right. I daresay your aunty will be after you. Well, you come back when you have an hour. And, mind, next time bring your sister. She'll like it particular."

Edmund thanked him and went off. But the thought of waiting alone in his room was too depressing. Besides, all he could think of was that if Mr. Dupin was wrong about this Mr. Fortnoy, perhaps it meant he was wrong about all the other things of which he'd been so sure.

Restless, Edmund began to wander aimlessly about the docks. There was enough to hold his interest. The on-and-off drizzle had brought a glossy wet shine to every surface. Flares burned with smoky fumes. Goods, coils of rope, piles of spars were everywhere. Now and again he chatted with men he had previously befriended. All had a kindly word. Many asked about his sister.

As he and Sis liked to do, Edmund began to search out interesting ship names. He found a fishing boat called *Sea Swan*, a coastal skiff named *Ebony*, and an old square-rigged merchant brig called *General Jackson*. Many a shared day-dream had begun with such names. Seeing them now made Edmund sad. He turned away.

With no fixed purpose in mind, Edmund made his way to the eastern end of the docks, around Fox Point, to the river wharfs where small fishing boats and ferries berthed. With weather so foul, work had ceased. And the longer Edmund wandered the more desolate the scene became. It matched his mood.

At last, he turned mournfully for home. But as he did he saw someone leap behind a stack of barrels. It was as if the person were trying to hide.

Edmund stood stock still, staring into the dark. Once again he recalled his notion that someone — or something — had followed him when he left his room the night before. And, yes, wasn't it the same, someone following Mr. Dupin as he went to Mrs. Whitman's just before? Now Edmund was not so ready to dismiss the idea.

Seeing nothing, he shifted his eyes. He realized suddenly just how alone he was. His apprehension grew. Then he checked himself. What had Mr. Dupin taught him? Be certain. He must be sure he was being followed.

Determined not to lose self-control, Edmund turned and continued along the deserted quay. To his left, across the river, city lights glowed. To the right rose College Hill, dark but for a few gas lamps. He saw no other person.

For a few more moments he went on, then abruptly stopped and spun about. A figure scurried behind a box. Was it, he wondered, someone intent upon stealing him as his sister had been stolen? Perhaps he would be taken to where she was. But what if she, like his aunt, had been murdered?

Trying to keep calm, Edmund spied a wharf which extended fifty or more yards into the river. It was, he saw, made of great crossed beams of wood, arranged trestle-fashion. Two boats were tied to it. Otherwise it appeared to be deserted.

An idea came to him. If he went out to the end of the wharf, the person following him, thinking him trapped, might follow further. And if he, Edmund, reached the wharf's end first, he also might go *under* the wharf, scramble beneath it, then come up *behind* the person and see just who it was.

Moving slowly, as though he were not being pursued, Edmund stepped onto the wharf. At the halfway point he halted and pretended to look at one of the two boats docked there. She was a small packet boat, a sloop which bore the name *Sunrise*. He stole a glance behind him. Through the murk he could just make out that whoever the stranger was, he *had* followed.

Fifteen yards from the end, Edmund paused again. He took a deep breath. After reminding himself what he was going to do, he took another breath, then burst into a run.

The moment he reached the wharf's end he threw himself down, then swiveled so as to let his legs dangle over the edge while his arms and hands, stretched to their limit, gripped the top surface planking. The wood was very splintery, and cut his fingers painfully.

Hand over hand, legs kicking madly, Edmund lowered himself into the inky blackness, each moment praying that his toes would find a crosspiece to settle on. His foot touched wood. Though he couldn't see the support he had to trust that it was wide enough, strong enough to hold him.

He swung in his other foot. It too found a surface. Held. Now, with both feet on the cross brace, he edged inward until he was standing firmly. The most difficult moment had come.

Wanting to ease down on the piece where his feet were resting so as to get *under* the wharf deck, Edmund knew he had to shift his grip. He must release his hold on the top with one hand then move that same hand down and grasp another support below. He made a tentative try, but he could not reach anything below the dock while simultaneously holding on to the top. His arms were too short. It was then that he realized he was going to have to let go of the top — completely — and allow himself to fall. He'd have a chance, one chance only, to make a snatch at a grip underneath. If he missed he'd be in the freezing black waters below.

His courage failed him. He could not do it. Frightened, he made an attempt to go back up. But he had gone too far. There was nothing to do but continue.

Swallowing hard, spreading his feet a little wider to gain more balance, heart racing madly, Edmund let go.

In the instant of falling from the wharf end he managed to shoot forward the hand already under the dock, swing down the other arm, then snatch at the wood with the tips of his fingers. The effort was just enough. He had grabbed hold of something. And he was quick enough to strengthen that small grip into a firmer hold. Though he had to gulp great drafts of air just to breathe, Edmund knew he was safe.

Even so there was no time to pause. It was impossible to know if the illusion he had meant to create — that of going off the wharf's end — had successfully fooled the person following him. Besides, even if he had succeeded, it meant only that the first part of his scheme had worked.

Like a monkey in a cage, Edmund scrambled beneath the dock. It was cold and slimy there. Masses of seaweed clung to the timbers around unexpected and painfully sharp clusters of barnacles. Still, he managed to move along the beams, over and under, until he was sure he was completely hidden.

He paused. Using his arms for balance, he was able to stand with some ease. As his breath returned to normal he attempted to look about. It was too dark. Instead he listened to the slap of water right below. The next moment he heard steps on the wharf deck directly overhead.

Crouching beneath the deck of the wharf, he listened as the footfalls passed and moved toward the end. There they stopped. Edmund held his breath. In moments the steps returned. Again they moved directly above him, then trailed back in the direction of the shore.

Sighing with relief, Edmund put the last part of his plan into action. He began to follow along the beams, hoping to see whoever it was.

He reached the shore end quickly. Once there he groped about for some way to get back to the top of the wharf. He was in luck. Where the wharf met the quay someone had built a crude ladder. He pulled himself up, poked his head out cautiously, and looked around.

At first it was too dark, too misty to see anything. And he heard not a sound. Then, gradually, some twenty feet away, he was able to make out what looked like the shadowy form of a man. But in the darkness all that Edmund could be sure of was a glow — rather like a halo — of white hair. *White hair.* Was it, he wondered with new excitement, Mr. Fortnoy?

Edmund searched for some way of getting closer. But before he could, the man began to move away until, to Edmund's dismay, he disappeared. All that was left was the sound of retreating footsteps.

Edmund allowed himself to relax. Though disappointed to have learned so little, he felt real satisfaction, even a little pride. He had not the slightest doubt that the stranger had followed him in order to take him, as he had taken Sis. On his own he had managed to avoid that.

Suddenly eager to tell Mr. Dupin what had happened, that — slight as his evidence was, he had after all learned something of Mr. Fortnoy — Edmund set off toward Mrs. Whitman's house.

15

THE FACE ON THE WALL

EDMUND STAMPED HIS feet, hoped it wouldn't rain again, and wondered what Mr. Dupin was doing inside Mrs. Whitman's house. Whatever it was, Edmund was sure the man was warmer than he was.

Thinking he could knock on the back door and ask Cook to allow him into the warm kitchen, Edmund started down the narrow side street. There he came upon the cemetery. It was the place, he remembered, where Mr. Dupin was to have met Mrs. Whitman.

Though it was difficult to see — the only light came from candles in the windows of the house — Edmund stood, one hand on the gate, and peered into the grave-yard. It didn't seem a suitable place for a meeting. But as he looked he gradually became aware of some kind of shimmering whiteness among the tombstones and brambles.

Puzzled, he finally realized it was a kneeling figure. For a moment Edmund believed that the person was digging, as if about to bury something. But he decided that was absurd. The person must be praying.

Not wanting to intrude, Edmund backed away. As he did the gate clinked. The noise caused the figure to jump up and stare in Edmund's direction.

At first the man — so blond that his hair seemed to be almost white — seemed startled to see Edmund. But the next moment he offered a cheerful look and a ready smile. "Hello," he said.

"I'm sorry to have bothered you," Edmund offered.

"Doesn't matter," the man said, approaching the gate. "I was finished."

"I'm just waiting for someone," Edmund explained.

The man's smile vanished. "Someone here?" he asked.

"In the house."

The man glanced at the building. Even as he did, the rear door opened and a knife of light cut across the cemetery.

"I must be going," the man said hastily. He pushed by Edmund and started up the hill, moving with such abruptness that a little book he'd been holding behind his back fell from his hand.

Edmund hurried to pick it up. When he did he saw that its cover was embossed with the words:

FIRST UNITARIAN CHURCH

141

"You dropped your prayer book!" Edmund called. The man, however, continued to hurry away.

Edmund was about to run after him when he looked toward Mrs. Whitman's house. Mr. Dupin had just emerged and was staring fixedly into the cemetery.

For a while Edmund watched the man closely, even followed his gaze. But when he saw nothing to warrant such rapt attention he called, "Mr. Dupin?"

Without replying or even acknowledging Edmund's presence, Dupin continued to stare.

"Mr. Dupin," Edmund said, drawing closer, "when I was at the dock I . . ."

Dupin cut him short. "Look over there," he said, pointing.

Edmund looked.

"What do you see?" Dupin demanded.

"The mausoleum."

"Edmund," Dupin said after a moment, "I want you to go inside it."

"Why?"

"You must tell me what you see."

"What's there?"

"Do as I say!" Dupin cried.

Suddenly anxious, Edmund stuffed the little prayer book into a pocket and made his way along the path to the mausoleum. At the steps he stopped and looked back. Mr. Dupin, watching intently, waved him on. Edmund went up the steps. Reaching the entrance, he halted and strained to see inside. The crypt was dank and dark and appeared to be empty.

Relieved, Edmund called back, "There's nothing here."

"Inside," Dupin insisted.

Edmund, feeling increasingly frustrated but wanting to placate Mr. Dupin so he could tell him about the wharf, took a step beyond the threshold. Still he saw nothing. He returned to the door.

"Anything?" Dupin asked.

Edmund shook his head.

"There has to be *something*."

"Mr. Dupin . . ."

"On the floor," Dupin suggested, "a mattress?"

"Nothing," Edmund assured him.

Dupin, his face broken by shadows, continued to stare at the mausoleum. Edmund came back to him. The light from the house revealed how haggard Mr. Dupin had become; his mouth was drawn, his brow furrowed, his eyes bloodshot.

"What is it?" Edmund asked.

When Dupin spoke he said, "I believe I have gone mad."

"What?" Edmund said.

"If it is a madness to see ghosts then . . . I am mad."

"What do you mean, ghosts? Whose ghost?"

Dupin looked at Edmund in such a way that the boy was seized with fright. "Is it my aunty's?" he asked in a hushed whisper. "My sister's?"

"The story is over," Dupin announced. *"Done."* Then, as

though coming back to life, he suddenly wheeled about, pushed past Edmund, and started down the hill.

Edmund called out, "Where are you going?"

"I must have a daguerreotype made," Dupin answered without pausing.

"Mr. Dupin!"

Dupin stopped and looked back.

"My sister isn't dead," Edmund insisted. *"She isn't!"*

"You are perfectly free to believe what you want," Dupin replied and once more turned down the hill.

Edmund ran after him. Though he raged, shouted, even pulled at Dupin's coat to detain him from going, the man refused to stop. He continued to march on, saying not a word as he reached the bottom of the hill, crossed the Providence River to the business section, and made his way up Weybosset Street.

Half a dozen times during this rapid walk Edmund came to a stop, determined to let Mr. Dupin go on. Each time, however, after watching Dupin disappear around a corner, he followed again. It was as if, by losing sight of him, Edmund would in some fashion acknowledge the truth of what Dupin had implied about his sister. He could not do it.

Dupin paused before the Providence Arcade. "I'm going in here," Dupin announced.

Edmund gazed at the huge stone columns looming over his head. "What for?" he asked, close to exhaustion.

"I'm in need of a portrait."

After checking a registry in the Arcade's central section, Dupin climbed two flights. Not understanding what the man was doing or why, but afraid that if he lost him it would be forever, Edmund kept a step behind.

On the top level Dupin went into a shop which bore the sign:

MASURY AND HARTSHORN STUDIO DAGUERREOTYPES

Inside, Edmund saw ferns, dark curtains, a large candelabra with none of its candles lit. Against one wall was a chair on a platform, and opposite, a big wooden box with a tube sticking out of it. The tube was pointed at the chair. Behind this machine was a wall covered with small portraits.

As soon as they entered the studio a formally dressed man, red-faced and with a large mustache, scurried out from a back room. " 'How do you do, sir," he said with a stiff bow. "I am Mr. Masury."

"I should like a portrait made," Dupin said.

"At your pleasure," Masury returned. "It will cost only a dollar."

Dupin paid and, after handing Edmund his greatcoat, allowed himself to be directed by Masury to the chair on the platform. There he took a seat and adjusted his cravat, making sure the top button of his jacket was open, while he buttoned the second.

"Very good," Masury said. "If you are thoroughly composed I shall make sure the plate is ready." He ducked behind the rear curtains.

Edmund took a seat off to the side, glad for the rest.

Masury returned and placed what looked like a thin box into the rear of the wooden machine. That done he hastened to light all the candles. They made the room as bright as day.

"Now, sir," he said to Dupin — by this time he was standing at the side of the box — "look this way. It will be necessary to hold still for an *entire* minute. If I may suggest it, set your gaze right over my shoulder. At these portraits, if you will. Are you ready, sir?"

"I am," Dupin replied, taking a breath.

"Eyes forward then," Masury called. "Ready, *start!*"

Dupin froze. He was, as Masury had told him to do, staring right at the portraits on the opposite wall.

As the count of seconds progressed Edmund saw Mr. Dupin grow pale. The man's hands clutched with tension. Beads of sweat gathered on his forehead. A look of undisguised horror came into his eyes.

Masury, unperturbed, monotonously continued counting. "Fifty-one, fifty two, fifty-three . . . *Done!*" he cried.

At the word Dupin leaped from the chair, took three steps across the floor, and pointed to one of the portraits on the wall.

"When was this made?" he cried.

Masury was so startled by the force of the question that he

almost dropped the box he had removed from the machine. "I must put this in the mercuralizer," he explained, "or the image will be lost."

Dupin reached out, grabbed the man's shoulder, and forced him to look. *"When was this made?"* he demanded a second time, jabbing a finger at a small portrait on the wall.

Thoroughly frightened, the man peered at the picture. "Why . . . months ago," he sputtered, then broke free of Dupin's grip and hurried behind the curtain as if his life depended upon it.

Dupin now turned on Edmund. "When did you come to Providence with your aunt?" he cried.

Edmund was too terrified to reply.

"Answer me!" Dupin shouted.

"A month ago," Edmund got out, shrinking back.

"Then who is this?" Dupin insisted, snatching at the boy with one hand, pointing toward the portrait with the other. *"Who is it?"*

Ready to bolt if Dupin became more violent, Edmund crept a step closer.

"Tell me!" Dupin shouted in a rage of impatience.

Edmund, trying to understand what Mr. Dupin was getting at, squinted at the picture. Suddenly he felt faint. "Why," he stammered, "it's my mother."

Dupin dropped his arm. "Your *mother?*" he cried. "I thought it was your *aunt.*"

Edmund kept staring at the portrait. "It is my mother," he said, finding it difficult to speak. "I know it is."

147

"But she looks exactly like your aunt," Dupin protested.

Edmund couldn't take his eyes from the image. "Not exactly. But they are twins."

"*Twins?*" Dupin gasped in a shocked whisper.

"Like Sis and me. I told you we were."

The whiteness of Dupin's face gave way to redness. "My God!" he cried. "*Twins!*"

"What's the matter with that?" Edmund demanded indignantly, unable to cope with yet another shift in the man.

At that moment Masury came out of the back room. "A few more minutes and it will be ready," he announced cheerfully.

"I can't wait," Dupin shouted. "I'll be back." Grabbing Edmund's hand, he rushed out the door.

"Your name, sir!" called Masury, following. "Your name!"

Dupin paused only long enough to call, "Poe! Mr. Edgar Allan Poe!" And down the steps he fled.

No matter how Edmund tried to make Dupin explain what he was doing — even what he meant by giving a different name — Dupin would not listen. Instead, he rushed back to the cemetery behind Mrs. Whitman's house. There, before the gate, he stopped.

"Now Edmund," he announced, struggling for breath, "we must look everywhere."

"What for?"

"I don't know," Dupin returned. "Something. Anything. It will be her. It must be! It has to be!"

Edmund gazed at him, baffled. Not that Dupin waited. He pushed through the gate and began to search wildly about the grounds. After a moment he looked back at Edmund. "Are you going to help or not?"

Though he had no idea what it was that he was supposed to find, Edmund started to search too.

Suddenly Dupin bent over. "Straw!" he cried out. "Straw from the mattress! Someone has removed and scattered it!" Immediately he turned to the mausoleum, went up the steps, pulled open the door, and stood looking in. Gingerly, Edmund followed.

"On your knees," Dupin commanded. "Feel around." Again Edmund held back. *"Do it!"* Dupin shouted at him as he himself crouched down on hands and knees. "Every inch."

In moments Dupin gave a triumphant cry. "There!" he shouted, picking up something and hurrying again to the doorway.

"What is it?" Edmund said behind him.

"Look!" Dupin said and thrust out his hand. In his palm lay a white button.

16

THE MAN WHO WAS POE

"MY SISTER'S!" EDMUND cried.

"Exactly," Dupin said. "Now come. We are done here."

As they hurried down Benefit Street toward the Fox Point district Edmund could hardly contain his excitement. "Mr. Dupin," he kept asking, "was my sister there?"

Dupin said nothing.

"Was she?"

Silence.

Edmund stopped short. He could bear it no longer. "Talk to me!" he shouted. "Tell me what you know!"

Dupin paused to look back where the boy was standing stubbornly. "Edmund, I am trying to think!"

"But it must have meant something. How did you know to look there?"

"It suggests but one thing: until very recently your sister was alive."

Edmund's breath felt sucked away. "Isn't she alive now?" he whispered.

Instead of answering, Dupin turned and continued on.

Edmund raced after him. "Is she?" he shouted, clutching hold of Dupin's arm.

Dupin jerked himself free and kept walking.

Something inside of Edmund broke. With a burst of rage he leaped in front of Dupin, preventing him from moving. "What did that daguerreotype tell you?" he cried. "I don't understand anything you say to me! You treat me well and then you speak and do awful things. I don't even know who you are or what your name is." He was screaming now, unable to stop the torrent of words and tears his anger spewed out.

"You drink so I can't tell whether to believe you or not. All I want is my sister and mother to be alive with me. Why do you keep scaring me? Why do you keep changing?" Spent, trembling, Edmund leaned against a building, pressed his burning face into his arms, and sobbed.

Dupin swore under his breath, then clumsily attempted to turn the boy from the wall.

Edmund shrugged him off. "Just tell me what you know," he sobbed.

"No matter how bad?"

Edmund pushed himself from the wall, wiped his face, and gazed at Dupin searchingly. "Is . . . is it bad?"

"I don't know," Dupin admitted. "Your aunt was murdered. I had believed your mother was too. And your sister as well."

"All three?" Edmund said, aghast.

"But what that daguerreotype told me was that your mother and your aunt were twins and looked alike."

"I don't think they do," a sniffling Edmund said.

"Do you recall what you said last night when you saw the body?"

Edmund shook his head.

"You said, *'It's not her dress.'* Edmund, I am no longer sure if that murdered woman was your aunt or your mother. What I *do* know is that one of them is alive."

"One of them?" Edmund cried, hardly able to speak.

"I have seen her."

"Where? When?" Edmund cried. "Why didn't you tell me?"

"Today . . . in the court. In the cemetery. Do they both have fair hair? A little shorter than I? Slender? Thin face?"

Edmund nodded to it all.

"I saw one of them."

"And my sister . . . ?"

"Did you do as I told you?" Dupin said by way of an answer. "Did you find out about that ship, *The Lady Liberty*?"

"Yes. But my sister . . ."

"And am I correct in believing there is *no* such ship, that all of that is a profound lie?"

Edmund shook his head. "Captain Elias said there is a *Lady Liberty*. From Nova Scotia, Halifax. She carries fish. Mr. Davis is her master. And that Mr. Fortnoy you spoke about, he's her watchman when she's in port. He'd been on her three days with no way to get off. Only when he was coming ashore did he find . . . that body."

Dupin stared at him. "Are you sure? Three days?"

"Captain Elias went to relieve him of his watch. Why did you need to know? And what does it have to do with Sis? Where is the woman you saw?" Edmund demanded.

Dupin, lost in thought, said nothing.

"Tell me!"

"I believed," Dupin replied, "there would be no such boat." So saying, he began to walk slowly away.

Edmund called out, "I was going to tell you something else."

Dupin stopped. "What is it?" he said in a gloomy, sulky voice.

Edmund told him about the man who had followed him at the docks and what he had done about it.

"Why didn't you tell me this before?" Dupin asked.

"You're just interested in your own thoughts."

"Nonsense! Did you see *who* the man was?" Dupin asked.

"Only that he had white hair. Do you think it was Mr. Fortnoy?"

"Edmund, are you absolutely positive your man said there's a ship called *The Lady Liberty* and that Fortnoy was on her for *three* days?"

"I don't lie," Edmund said.

Dupin let out his breath. "I need a drink," he said, and began walking again.

"Tell me more about the woman you saw!" Edmund screamed at him.

When Dupin kept walking Edmund ran after him. "Mr. Dupin, we have to find Sis."

"I work better with drink," Dupin murmured.

"When you drink you act badly."

Dupin swung about in anger. "Edmund," he cried, "lead me to a place where I can drink!"

"Tell me about the woman you saw!"

For a moment the two confronted each other, gazing into one another's eyes. Edmund saw a terrible sadness there. "Who are you?" he asked. "What is your real name?"

"Poe. Edgar Allan Poe."

"Why is it a secret?"

"Edmund," Dupin pleaded, "what does it matter?"

"But . . . what shall I call you?"

"I am . . . the man who *was* Poe. Now I am Dupin. And I must have a drink. It eases the pain."

"What pain?"

"The pain of living when those you love have died."

"Mr. Poe . . ."

"Don't call me that!" Dupin cried out in horror.

"Mr. Dupin, if I take you to the saloon will you tell me what you know about the woman you saw?"

"Yes."

Edmund led the way to the small saloon near his room. The air there, heavy with rum, seemed oppressively hot. They took a table as far as possible from the corner stove.

The bearded counter man watched them suspiciously. Edmund looked for the night watchman but couldn't find him.

"You must be hungry," Dupin said. "Is this where you got the meat pie last night? Do you wish one?" He offered Edmund some coins. "You can get me a rum."

Edmund, depressed at the thought of Dupin drinking again, shook his head. "The woman," he said. "You promised."

Dupin put a hand over his eyes. "Edmund, I am trying to finish the story."

"I don't believe you."

"I am a writer," Dupin said. "A great one."

"You are a drunkard," Edmund returned, feeling only disgust. "And you were not telling the truth about seeing a woman, were you?"

Dupin shook his head. "You don't understand. Lies have their own truth."

"Then tell me!"

"A drink . . ."

Edmund took the money and requested the rum. It was given him in a filthy glass. Dupin took it greedily.

Unable to watch, Edmund moved away. As he tried to quell the feeling of anger and contempt churning inside, he examined the wall of bills and posters. It was then that he noticed one bill in particular.

"Mr. Dupin!" he cried.

When Dupin paid no attention Edmund yanked the bill

off the wall and thrust it into his hand, then stood behind the man while he read:

REWARD

Persons providing information leading to the
finding of one Mrs. G. Rachett, of London,
England, but believed to be a recent resident
of Providence, Rhode Island, shall be entitled
to a bonded reward. Please contact Mr. Poley,
Providence Bank, South Main, at
earliest convenience.
Oct. 15, 1848

"That's my mother," Edmund said, pointing to the name. "Mrs. G. Rachett."

"This must have been your aunt's bill," Dupin murmured as he read. Then suddenly he cried, "Good Lord!" And Edmund heard him whisper. "Mr. *Poley!*"

"Who?"

"The man at the bank."

"What bank?" Edmund asked, moving around the table. As he watched, a transformation took place. Mr. Dupin's eyes lightened. His face cleared. Suddenly, he reached out, and catching Edmund by surprise, took tight hold of his shoulders. "You said you did not know what your step-father, Mr. Rachett, looked like. Are you absolutely certain of that?"

"I didn't know," Edmund said, "but this afternoon when you went to Mrs. Whitman, I followed you and . . ."

"Followed me? Why?"

"I didn't think you were telling me the truth."

Dupin glowered, then said, "Go on with what you were saying."

"Just after you went to the cemetery, Mrs. Whitman's maid rushed out of the house. It made me wonder — she had acted angry with me, and even Mrs. Whitman seemed fearful of her — so I followed. She went to a hotel."

"Which one?"

"Hotel American House."

"What happened next?" Dupin cried excitedly.

"She returned with a man to the house."

"And the man . . . ?"

"The one you said was Mr. Rachett."

"Describe him!"

Edmund did.

For a moment Dupin just stared at the boy. Then he said, "Edmund, did I not tell you when this began that you held the answers which would resolve this matter? Did I not?"

"Yes . . ."

"In Providence, Edmund, that man you saw goes by the name of Mr. William Arnold."

"Mr. Dupin," Edmund cried, "there was a Mr. Arnold in Mrs. Whitman's house this morning."

157

"Explain!"

"When I went to deliver your message this morning I got lost in the house and came up against a door. I heard people talking on the other side. I didn't know it then because I didn't know your true name, but they must have been talking about you."

"What were they saying?"

"First a woman spoke," Edmund said. "I think it was a Mrs. Powers. She was telling this man, Mr. Arnold, how bad you were, and that they must stop Mrs. Whitman from being with you. She wanted Mr. Arnold to marry her."

"Motive, Edmund, *motive*!" Dupin cried with glee. "Continue."

"And the man agreed. But I didn't understand any of it," Edmund said.

"But I do!" Dupin cried. Grabbing the bill, he leaped up from the table and rushed to the counter. "Do you know Mr. Throck?" he demanded of the man.

Startled, the counter man looked up. "Throck?" he echoed.

"Yes! Throck. Of the night watch."

The man grew cautious. "What makes you ask?"

"Does he take private cases?"

"He may or may not . . ."

Dupin slammed his fist down on the counter. "Tell me!"

The counter man jumped. "I suppose he does."

Dupin thrust the bill at him. "This one?"

"Well, yes, that one . . ."

"Of course he took his one!" cried Dupin. "Once I promise to find a thing I see it through!" Dupin whirled about to face Edmund. "The man at the wharf — the man who threatened you — what did you say you noticed about him?"

"His hair."

"What about it?"

"It was white."

"*White.* Yes, of course!" he cried out. "Of course! To your room, Edmund," he called. "Hurry!"

Edmund, galvanized by Dupin's burst of energy, led the way out onto the dark street.

As they rushed forward, thunder and lightning crashed above them and a freezing rain began. More than once Dupin stumbled on the slippery pavement.

Edmund reached the alleyway leading to his door first. He stopped and looked back. Dupin was some twenty paces behind. Concerned that Dupin would miss the turning in the dark, the boy waited and watched. And as he did, he saw a large man step swiftly out from beneath the shadow of an archway, lift an arm, and extend it toward Dupin. A bolt of lightning lit the sky. In the flash Edmund saw the man was holding a pistol.

"Mr. Dupin!" Edmund shouted, at the same time flinging himself at the man. The man whirled, struck at Edmund with the pistol, and sent him crashing to the ground. Again the man turned toward Dupin. Dupin, however, was now only a few feet away, and charging. His greatcoat was off, and the next moment he swung it toward the man as though it were a net. Taken by surprise, the man was forced to back up a step.

Edmund attempted to snatch at the man's legs. Trying to avoid both Dupin and Edmund, the man lurched to one side and jerked up his hand. Dupin dove to the muddy ground. A shot exploded.

"Mr. Dupin!" Edmund screamed. As he pulled himself up, lightning flashed again, shedding just enough light for him to see Mr. Rachett running down the street.

Dupin struggled to a sitting position. "Did you see who it was?" he called.

"The man you said was Rachett," said Edmund, trying to get his breath back.

Dupin grunted. "I should have anticipated him."

"Did he hit you?"

"I managed to throw his aim off. Where are we?" he asked. "Give me a hand."

"My room is just here," Edmund said, helping Dupin to his feet and gesturing to the alley.

"Continue!"

As if even further excited by his brush with death, Dupin moved quickly to Edmund's room. Once there he demanded a candle. Edmund found one, then lit it. And Dupin began a frantic search.

"What are you looking for?" Edmund asked wearily. He had caught sight of Dupin's eyes, which seemed to have grown unnaturally brilliant.

Dupin looked around. "That meat pie was wrapped in

newspaper. Edmund, if you wish this story to have an end help me find it!"

"It's not a story," Edmund objected, beginning to wonder if the man had been made unstable by the attack. But when Dupin commenced to search again he joined him — and found the crumpled newspaper in a corner. "Is this what you want?" he asked in a truculent voice.

Dupin snatched the paper from Edmund's hand, glanced at it, and gave it back. "Read those notices," he insisted, pointing to several advertisements.

Edmund eyed Dupin, then began to read:

"NOTICE EXTRAORDINARY
As this is the season when Game —"

"The last one!" Dupin snapped.

"POSITION WANTED
The advertiser, R. Peterson, a good copyist and
accountant, thoroughly discreet, being at leisure
from 6 to 9 P.M. Would like any re . . ."

Edmund turned to Dupin.
"Re-mun-er-a-tive," Dupin said. "Means paying."

". . . munerative employment three or four evenings
a week. Apply at Providence Bank office for
particulars."

"Now the one before that," Dupin said.

Again Edmund read.

"NOTICE

Mr. William Arnold is resident in the Hotel
American House on Congdon Street, and is
ready to conduct business with interested
parties. Principals only."

"There, you see!" Dupin said. "I was right."

"Mr. Dupin . . ."

"What?"

"After I heard that conversation in Mrs. Whitman's house, I went through the door and found some writing on the floor. I think one of the people must have dropped it. But I didn't know what it meant."

"What did you do with it?"

Edmund thought, took up his sister's book, and pulled out the paper with the odd symbols on it.

Dupin examined it. As he did his face went absolutely pale. "Good God!" he whispered.

"What is it?"

"*I* wrote that!" Dupin exclaimed.

Edmund, convinced Mr. Dupin *had* gone mad, looked at him with dismay.

" 'The Gold Bug,' " Dupin said.

"The *what*?"

"Edmund, I am the most famous writer in America. One

of the tales I wrote is called 'The Gold Bug.' The story contains a code, and this message is written in that code."

"What does it say?"

Dupin held up the note and read slowly:

"Meet me at the hotel. I have moved girl and gold. Must leave. Sunrise at six A.M."

Edmund's heart skipped a beat. "Does he mean my sister?" he cried.

Dupin held up his hand. "Give me ten minutes."

"But . . ."

"Ten minutes!" Dupin insisted.

With a cry of frustration Edmund retreated to the bed, sat down with his back against the wall, and stared angrily at Dupin. The time dragged interminably. Now and again Edmund dabbed at his wet clothing or hair with the blanket. Dupin continued to stand where he was, eyes aflame. At last he said, "Yes, I understand it all."

17

NO DETAIL TOO SMALL

"ARE YOU GOING to tell me?" Edmund asked.

Instead of answering, Dupin sat at the table. From his pocket he removed a string and set it before him. Next to that he placed a card, as well as the message Edmund had found. Finally, he laid out the two white buttons. In the light of the candle they glowed like pearls.

"Edmund," he said, "you must listen with the utmost care. As I link detail to detail I shall be speaking as much to myself as to you. No detail is too small. Is that understood?"

"Yes, but . . ."

"Then do not interrupt me!" Dupin took a deep breath. "A while ago," he began in a voice trembling with excitement, "your mother is abandoned by your stepfather, Rachett. Not just abandoned. He steals her money. I wouldn't be surprised if she were not the only one he so abused.

"Rachett has used your mother's money to insinuate himself into the regard of one Mrs. Powers, a woman well placed in the city of Providence. Both vicious and cautious, he has taken on the name of William Arnold. Arnold is an old, respected family name in this city.

"In time your mother discovers that he has come here, to Providence. Seeking a return of her money as well as a divorce — not obtainable in England — she sails in search of him, leaving you in the charge of her twin sister, your aunt Pru.

"After not hearing from your mother for a year, your aunt suddenly receives a message from her. A *message* — as opposed to a letter — brought moreover by a stranger — tells me that your mother is under restraint, perhaps even held captive by Rachett.

"The urgency of your mother's message, the very means of delivery, causes your aunt to come immediately to Providence, bringing you and your sister with her. Once here she commences her search. Do I make sense so far?"

"I suppose."

"Not long after your arrival," Dupin raced on, "your aunt asks the Providence Bank to help her in her search by offering a reward. The notice posted in the saloon proves she spoke to Mr. Poley.

"Throck — you remember him —"

Edmund nodded.

"— sees that notice and engages with your aunt to find your mother. The man in the saloon confirms this. Throck

165

himself told me as much himself this morning. Thinking I was after the reward, he even tried to warn me off. 'Meddle at your peril!' he informed me. A distraction.

"Meanwhile," Dupin continued, "at the bank, Mr. Poley talks about your aunt and her affairs. The workers in his office overheard. One of these is Mr. Randolf Peterson."

"Who's he?" Edmund asked.

"The accountant who published that advertisement in the newspaper." Dupin pointed to the card that lay before him.

Edmund got up off the bed to read it.

MR. RANDOLF PETERSON
Hotel American House

"Rachett," Dupin continued, "must have seen that notice too and thus learned of your aunt's arrival. Wishing to see if she knows his *false* name he places *his* advertisement in the paper. Naturally, he checks the paper to see that it is there. In so doing he sees Peterson's advertisement which appears the same day.

"Rachett, deciding he must do something about your aunt, approaches Peterson. What could be easier? They *live in the same place*. Peterson not only tells Rachett about your aunt's dealings at the bank, he mentions the California gold."

"At the bank?" Edmund said.

"Exactly. Rachett is deeply interested in both pieces of news," Dupin intoned, as if he were in a trance. "Remember, he has met Mrs. Powers and through her, Mrs. Whitman, whom he has determined to marry. To do so he needs two things. He must rid himself of his legal wife, your mother. Divorcing her will not do. Mrs. Powers will not condone it. He also needs money to appear a worthy prospect.

"The coming of your aunt with the two of you, in conjunction with the arrival of the California gold, *and* the willingness of Peterson to involve himself in a robbery, work together in Rachett's mind. He constructs a monstrous plot. To begin with, Peterson becomes his partner."

Dupin stood and for a moment began to pace. Edmund watched him intensely.

"It is easy," Dupin at last continued, "for Peterson to learn from Mr. Polcy where your aunt has taken a room. The first thing Rachett does is engage a room opposite you." Dupin pointed out the window.

"Then he schemes to get hold of your aunt. You told me that just before she disappeared, she was to meet a man. Correct?"

Edmund nodded.

"Rachett or Peterson. They lure your aunt away, with the promise of information about your mother.

"Now Rachett holds *both* your mother and your aunt. And he determines to murder your mother. Why not destroy the aunt too? Rachett, a cautious man, does *nothing* in excess. Do what must be done. No more. Indeed, I'd wager that it is Peterson, not Rachett, who actually does the deed.

"In any case, it is my belief that your mother and aunt

discover the plot. To thwart such a despicable plan, to protect you children, the sisters — identical twins — exchange places and thus confound the murderers. For indeed one of the sisters *is* killed and thrown into the bay.

"Rachett and Peterson believe they have killed your mother. In fact, your aunt has sacrificed herself for motherhood.

"But on the night of the robbery, while Rachett and Peterson are otherwise occupied, the surviving sister escapes. Ever since, she has been trying to find *your* sister, and, no doubt, you. Terrified, grief-stricken, hardly knowing where to go, she wanders the city in search of her children. Poor woman, she is all but mad.

"No, don't say a word!" Dupin cried. "I now return to Rachett and Peterson. Why did they desire to secure your aunt? Because with her gone you and your sister will be left alone.

"With the patience of Satan, the two men wait in that room opposite yours for one of you to leave. Ah! But from later events — the breaking into the room — we know they have a key. Why not use it then? Because the window is the fastest way to secure the child. After all, who knows when the one who leaves will return? Secrecy, mystification, specd, all essential!

"In any case it is you, Edmund, who at last gocs out for food. Now then, did you not say you were detained on the street that night?"

"Yes."

"By whom?"

"An old man."

"How did you know he was old?"

"He acted old and . . ."

Dupin slammed his hand on the table, making Edmund jump. *"He had white hair!* In fact, it is young Mr. Peterson who detains you so that Rachett can steal your sister!"

"Why?"

"The bank, Edmund! The bank! To get the gold in the Providence Bank. There is an air shaft in that bank vault where the shipment has been placed. It leads to the roof. The roof abuts the hill behind it. There is an alley alongside. Drive a carriage into the alley and it is a small matter to climb upon the roof and reach the opening.

"However, while no grown person can go down through that shaft, a *child*, Edmund, a child you or your sister's size could be lowered down by rope."

"Down the shaft?" Edmund gasped, horrified.

"Exactly. And I have no doubt that if it had been your sister who had gone to the store they would have taken you and done the same."

Edmund paled.

Dupin crossed to the table, picked up the piece of string that lay there and dangled it before Edmund's eyes. "I found this in the vault," he said, "and compared it with the bell ropes in the Unitarian Church. It is not string, but a piece of strong *rope.*

"Individually, the bars of gold are not that heavy. A child —

169

in this case your sister — could place them, one by one, into a basket that is lowered with her, and then . . . all are hauled away.

"Do you not see Edmund, the women in this story, the women who are not here — are everywhere!

"Indeed, your sister herself has a means of thwarting these men. A plucky girl, she takes it from that story she's read, 'Hansel and Gretel.'" Dupin flung the string aside and scooped up the buttons. "Your sister leaves a button everywhere she is taken.

"Peterson, with the bragging vanity of the thief, shows me one he himself found in the bank, little knowing what I know.

"The robbery done," Dupin continued, "the men hide your sister in the abandoned cemetery behind Mrs. Whitman's house — in the mausoleum. This second button here proves that.

"Rachett — pretending to be Arnold — has been to the house often in pursuit of Mrs. Whitman. He believes the mausoleum is never visited.

"In any case, all has gone as planned — except the woman they think is your aunt has escaped. Are they greatly concerned? No! What can your aunt do to them? A foreigner. A woman. A spinster. It would be her word against Rachett, who, as I told you, under the name Arnold, has allied himself with powerful friends of Mrs. Powers in this city.

"Ah, but something of great importance happens.

Something Rachett or Peterson could hardly have foreseen. You meet *me*! And I, as Auguste Dupin, undertake to unravel the mystery.

"Now, Edmund, this morning, under my direction, you go into a clothing store. Rachett sees you. Edmund, these are the crucial moments. Consider how his mind must have worked.

"*One!* He sees you, recognizes you, and is struck by your similarity to your sister.

"*Two!* That reminds him of how much alike were your mother and aunt.

"*Three!* Suddenly he asks himself, did we kill the right woman? Could it be that it is my wife who escaped?

"*Four!* Unable to be certain he becomes panicked.

"*Five!* He must find the truth!

"*Six!* He rushes to this room, and discovers that picture in the trunk.

"*Seven!* The picture only incites his worst fears: they may have done away with, not your mother but your aunt!

"Now then, given that, we deduce his state of mind: all is placed in jeopardy. Rachett knows he must escape. But he needs to make certain he's left no evidence behind. He rushes to the mausoleum and retrieves your sister.

"He then writes a message. He knows my work. Brags of it. Has read, 'The Gold Bug,' as has Peterson. Lazy man, he uses the code in my story to write to Peterson."

From the table Dupin picked up the message Edmund had found and read it out loud:

"Meet me at the hotel. I have moved girl and gold. Must leave. Sunrise at six A.M.

"But, before Rachett can deliver this, Mrs. Powers observes him in the cemetery and detains him. That's when you overhear the conversation. Rachett drops the message.

"Leaving Mrs. Powers he must send another message to Peterson. They meet and make plans. *At the hotel.* While Arnold goes to the tea party — he cannot refuse Mrs. Powers — Peterson is to do two things: clean out the mausoleum, then secure you."

"Me?"

"Of course. If they have both you and your sister, your mother will have that much less of a hold on Rachett. And it is you, Edmund, who make it easy for them to try."

"What do you mean?"

"Did you not say you followed me to Mrs. Whitman's and then the maid to the Hotel American House?"

"Yes, but . . ."

"What happened next?"

"I followed her and Mr. Rachett back to Mrs. Whitman's house."

"And then?"

"I went to the docks."

"Don't you see? Peterson — in the hotel — must have seen you and followed you all the way."

Edmund's mouth dropped open.

"Meanwhile, I go to my meeting with Mrs. Whitman in the cemetery. When I do, I see a person resembling the dead woman I've seen in the court of inquest. I see her coming out of the mausoleum. I believe it to be the ghost of your aunt.

"Now then, only when I see the daguerreotype do I realize there are *two* women who look alike. Understanding that, I know I have *not* seen a ghost. I am not mad. It is something more extraordinary than that. I have made a mistake!

"No, the woman I saw was either your unfortunate mother or your aunt looking for you and your sister.

"One further point. At Mrs. Whitman's, I unknowingly alluded to the incident at the clothier. Rachett, hearing me, believes I know the truth, though in fact, at that moment, I do not. But when he rushes out and comes to wait near this building prepared to kill me it provides the final proof that I have thought it all out properly. Now, no doubt, at this very moment, he is preparing to flee the city!"

"With Sis?"

Dupin, exhausted, sat down at the table. "I don't know," he said.

"But who was killed? My mother or my aunt?"

Dupin shrugged.

Edmund said, "Captain Elias told me he saw someone this morning on the docks who looked like Aunty. He told her about the inquest."

"The woman I saw."

"And another thing," Edmund said, becoming more and more excited. "It's about the cemetery."

"What is that?"

"Just before I found you at Mrs. Whitman's there was a man there."

"Hair so blond as to be almost white?" said Dupin wearily. "Bright blue eyes, and round, red cheeks."

Edmund nodded.

"*That* is your Mr. Peterson. More confirmation of what I've been saying. Failing to murder you, Peterson returns to the cemetery for a final clearing out of the mausoleum."

"I thought he was praying," Edmund said. "He dropped this." Edmund took out the prayer book and offered it to Dupin.

Dupin considered the book, then flipped it onto the table.

"Doesn't that tell you anything?" Edmund asked, disappointed.

"Left by the woman I saw. She must have gotten it from the Unitarian Church. They allow the homeless to sleep there. It suggests she may well be there now."

"*Now?*"

"Yes, of course." Dupin reached into his carpetbag and removed notebook, pen, and ink bottle.

"But . . . Mr. Dupin . . ."

"That's not my name."

"*What?*"

"My name is Poe. Edgar Allan Poe."

"Mr. . . . Poe, aren't we going?"

"Going? Going where?"

"To the church."

"Why should we?"

"You just said my mother or my aunt might be there! And maybe Sis, too."

Poe shook his head even as he opened his notebook. "As far as I'm concerned they are all dead."

Edmund, shocked, stared at him. "But they *aren't* dead. You just said so."

"In *my* story they will die." Poe dipped his pen into the ink bottle.

Edmund gazed at the man in disbelief. "Mr. Dupin —"

"*Poe!*"

"Mr. Poe, this *isn't* a story."

Poe, poised to write, gave a shake of his head. "Edmund, I should really appreciate it if you would go back to that saloon and get me some drink. I never quite finished." He laid some coins on the table.

Edmund felt weak.

"Believe me," Poe continued, "I have done more for you than any other human could have done. Now, I have my work to do."

"*But, we have to find them!*" Edmund cried.

"Edmund, I am a writer, not an adventurer. My function is to think and then to write about what I think. Must I repeat myself? I'm no longer concerned with *your* story. As for *my* story, I have a more elaborate ending to pursue. Didn't you hear me? Can't you understand? I'm no longer Auguste Dupin. I am the man who *is* Edgar — Allan — Poe."

Edmund stood still, staring at Poe as he bent over his notebook, writing. "But . . ."

"Boy, is this the thanks I get for solving your problem? Go."

After a moment Edmund stepped forward, placed the money on the table, then turned and went out.

Poe lifted his head and listened to Edmund walk down the hallway. When he heard the hall door open and close, he sighed, put down his pen, and took up the money. Next he put on his greatcoat. Then he too left the room.

18

THE WOMAN IN THE CHURCH

EDMUND DASHED OUT onto the dark street. Rain was pelting down. Street gutters ran with foam and filth. Gusts of wind hurled fists of water against walls, rattled signs, and pulled doors open, only to bang them shut. The few people abroad, their collars up, hats low, hurried by.

As if trying to outrun the rain, Edmund bolted for Benefit Street and did not stop running until he reached the Unitarian Church.

The church was an enormous white stone building whose steeple, towering high, seemed to melt into the dismal murk above. Over its door a lamp — swinging wildly in the wind — was lit. The light it cast on the church's white porch made Edmund think of a pile of dancing bones.

Panting for breath, soaked to the skin and shivering, he hastened up the walkway and tried the central entry. When it didn't yield, he went on to the side door. That was open.

As large as the building looked from outside, it seemed bigger within. Its central hall was huge, its pulpit massive. From the ceiling hung an enormous chandelier jeweled with a few small candles whose flames fluttered like pale butterfly wings.

Edmund ventured down the center aisle. Most of the main floor was covered with pews. And he could make out a grand balcony on three sides with more rows of pews. All had polished rails. Tucked behind the rails were prayer books like the one he had found.

Edmund stood and listened to the sounds of the storm outside. The rain, pounding above, echoed the beating of his heart. Gradually he began to hear sighing, muttering, deep breathing. As his eyes became adjusted to the gloom he saw that here and there people were huddled, seeking sanctuary from the rain and cold, hunched over as if in hiding.

Then Edmund heard a low moaning sound close to the pulpit. At first he thought it was only the wind. But when it came again he realized it was human.

He edged nearer. Someone lay curled against the pulpit. Gradually he saw that it was a woman and she was wearing a faded, torn gown of striped white and pale green. "Aunty!" he cried out.

The woman did not move.

Heart pounding, Edmund drew closer and knelt down, trying to see the woman's face. At first all he could see was that it was shabby, tear-streaked. Then he saw more.

"Mother . . . ?" he began.

The moaning ceased. The figure stirred. Slowly she turned toward him. "Who is it?" she asked.

"It's me . . . Edmund . . ."

The woman pushed the hair out of her face. The face was thin and filthy, her eyes dark and disbelieving. *"Edmund?"* she whispered.

He nodded.

Her lips trembled. "Alive?"

"Yes."

She reached out slowly and gently touched his face, letting her fingers linger. Then she withdrew her hand, turned from him and looked around the church as if to reassure herself about where she was. Again she turned and fastened her gaze on Edmund.

"I was not sure . . . I'd see you again."

"I'm here."

"So much . . . bigger."

He nodded tearfully.

She held out her arms. For a long time they cradled each other. Neither spoke. Outside the wind and rain continued.

Finally Edmund said, "Can you tell me what happened?"

"I'll . . . try." Haltingly, sometimes groping for words, Mrs. Rachett told her son the story.

"After coming to Providence it was quite a while before I found Mr. Rachett. He'd taken the name of Arnold and — with my money — was living the life of a proper gentleman. When I made myself known to him he was furious, said I'd ruined *his* life. That was his way.

179

"I told him I wanted but two things: a divorce and the return of my money.

"The divorce he'd give, he said at first, but not the money.

"On my part I'd not give him one without the other. It was the only hold I had.

"He accused *me* of causing scandal! Whatever he could blame others for, or get others to do for him, that was his way. To be seen as gentry, *that* was what was important to him.

"In fearing I should expose him, he lured me with a promise that I should have what I wanted, then kept me virtual prisoner for months. Oh, anything to have the world think him a proper gentleman!

"I wrote a message to my sister, your Aunt Pru, begging her for help. But how could I get it to her? By then I had no money of my own at all. Still, I carried that message about me so — on the rare occasion he let me out with him — a chance might offer itself. Sure enough, once when I was momentarily alone I spied a British sailor. I gave the message to him and begged him to deliver it. He said he would if he could.

"He must have done. For Pru did come, bringing you. I don't know how, but Mr. Rachett learned of her arrival. And in the meanwhile he'd decided to marry a wealthy widow by the name of Mrs. Whitman. The achievement of all his desires. Ever greedy, he planned a crime, which I learned required the use of my children!

"I told him then — begged him — to let me go. I'd make no claims to the money. Alas, it was too late for that.

"First he found a way to get hold of Pru. Oh, Edmund, she and I had a painful reunion. Worse, when Mr. Rachett demanded her room key we were in dreadful fear that he intended to use you and your sister in some life-threatening way we could not grasp. And then, there was our gradual awareness that he had the most dreadful designs on me, his wife.

"For Mr. Rachett had taken on a partner, a young man called Peterson. A vicious man, he was always egging Mr. Rachett on to violence. One night we overheard Peterson urging him to kill us both. The two men argued. Mr. Rachett, squeamish in his evil way, said it need only be one — me, his wife.

"It was my sister Pru who — in a desperate scheme to thwart their plans — conceived the idea of our changing clothes so as to confuse them. She would sacrifice herself while I — your mother — would at least have the chance to save you. Reluctantly, I agreed. The trick worked. It was your Aunt Pru who was led away by Peterson.

"But as Pru was taken away Mr. Rachett warned me, whom he thought to be Pru, that if I got up to any mischief, the children's lives would be forfeit.

"That same night I escaped. But I was so horrified by my husband's final, fearful threat, that though free, I felt lost, unsure of where to turn. I did make my way to the church where I slept some, and prayed.

"Next morning, I was so distracted that I could not recollect where it was that Pru had said she'd taken a room. I knew only it was by the docks. There, in search of you children, I went. At the docks I learned for certain of my sister's death. I went to the inquest. More frightened than ever, I ran from the place.

"Chance brought me to see Peterson outside the bank. He was talking to a man, but then Peterson set off up College Hill. I followed.

"Peterson stopped to turn into a cemetery and entered a small mausoleum. While I watched he soon emerged and hurried on. Suspicious, I followed his tracks. In the mausoleum — though it was deserted — I found evidence that someone had been held there. I was certain it was my children.

"It was then that another man discovered me, the same one I had seen Peterson talking to outside the bank. But when I saw he was not alone, I fled. In despair I crept back to the church."

The rest Edmund knew.

He in turn told his mother what had happened during the year they had been apart. He told her how Sis had been stolen and about her terrifying role in the robbery, and how he had been searching and searching for her.

Finally his mother said, very quietly, "Edmund, do you think your sister is alive?"

At first he hesitated, then nodded.

"But . . . where is she?"

"I'll find her," Edmund declared as, gently, he helped her to her feet and down the aisle of the church.

PART THREE

19

THE STORY

IT WAS NIGHT. There was a man. There was a boy. And they moved through the city with grim determination, uncertain of their fate, uncertain of the fate of those they sought. . . . Poe, sitting at the table, writing in his notebook by the light of a small candle, could see them distinctly. Two empty bottles lay at his feet. A third bottle, almost empty, was near at hand.

And he could hear the characters too. "I found her," one of them said.

Poe wrote that down, then frowned. It didn't feel right.

The voice came again. It was more insistent than before. "Mr. Poe, I found her."

Poe looked up. It was very dim in the room and at first he wasn't sure what he was seeing. Gradually he began to see that it was the boy from his story standing before him. He was dripping wet. Behind him stood someone who appeared — Poe was not sure at first — to be a woman. She was dressed in dirty clothes and was in an advanced state of exhaustion. It was as if she had traveled some immense distance.

Poe stared at the two of them, then looked down into his notebook and read what he had been writing, only to look up again with a start. A thrill of excitement passed through him. The characters he'd been writing about had actually come to life. They were standing before him! Never in all his years had he had such a vivid sense of the reality of his own creations.

"At the church," the boy said.

"I am not surprised," Poe murmured, delighted that these characters of his were speaking their own lines. It was so much easier than having to struggle to find the words himself.

The boy turned, and under Poe's fascinated gaze, helped the woman to the bed, where she lay down. She sighed and closed her eyes. The boy took a place near her on the edge of the bed.

Poe smiled. It was his dream come true. He needed only to look at these images, watch what they did, and describe them on the page. For a while he studied the two. Then he bent over his notebook and wrote:

The boy turned and helped the woman to the bed, where she lay down. She sighed and closed her eyes. The boy took a place near her on the edge of the bed.

"Did you buy food?" came a voice.

Poe, without looking up from his writing, shook his head. "Only a necessary drink," he said softly and to no one in particular. He wasn't sure who had spoken.

"Please give me money. I need to get her some food."

"I am trying to write," Poe said.

"Please, she needs it very badly."

Poe looked about, surprised to find that the boy character had drawn very close. Then to his horror he saw the boy reach out for the bottle. Before the boy could grasp it, Poe himself snatched it from the table and hugged it to his body.

Warily, Poe studied the boy's face. Now he was no longer certain it was his character. But then who was it? Just the thought made his head ache.

"Do you know who I am?" the boy asked.

"Yes."

"Who?"

Poe thought carefully before answering. Puzzling questions, he reminded himself, are not beyond *all* conjecture. He studied the boy's face carefully. Even as he did a name came into his mind. But he rejected that name as not right. He tried another. "Is it," he said, "Edmund?"

"Yes."

Poe grunted with satisfaction. "The other boy is better," he said. "He does what he is told to do."

"What other boy?"

Poe put a hand to his head. "The one here. His name is —"

"Mr. Dupin —"

Poe slammed his fist on the table. *"Poe!"* he cried.

"Please . . ."

Poe closed his eyes. When he opened them he saw that boy, Edmund, standing there, waiting. Grudgingly he reached into a pocket and dragged forth some coins and held them out. When Edmund took them Poe turned to look at the bed. The woman was still there. But the other character was gone. Annoyed, he bent over his writing again and tried to recapture the vision.

*   *   *

Edmund glanced at his mother, trying to make up his mind if he dared leave her. She was asleep. He studied Poe. Edmund was not at all certain the man really knew who he was. At the moment he seemed to be utterly absorbed in his work.

"I'm going to get some food," Edmund announced.

Poe said nothing.

"I'll be right back."

Edmund left the room, shut the door behind him, then paused to listen. When he heard the steel pen scratching across the paper he took one step only to stop, put his key in the lock, and turn it. Mr. Poe would not be able to get out.

Suddenly Edmund was caught up in a memory of the last time he'd locked the door. For a second he had the distinct sensation that he was seeing himself in some story. What would happen, he wondered, if he opened the door again. Would Sis be there this time? With a shake of his head, he cleared his head of the foolish thought and moved toward the stairs.

When he walked into the saloon Mr. Throck was laying

cards out on the table for a game of solitaire. At first he gave
the boy no more than a quick glance. But when he realized
it was Edmund, he stared at the newcomer.

The man behind the counter looked down. "Yes, boy," he
said gruffly. "What do you want?"

"Please, sir," Edmund said, dumping Mr. Poe's coins on
the counter, "a meat pie. And candles."

"Large pie or small?"

"This is the money I have, sir."

The man made a slow count of the coins. "Four candles
and a large pie," he said, taking up the money.

While the counter man got his purchase ready Edmund
stole a glance at Throck.

"What are you looking at?" the big man growled.

"Are you Mr. Throck?" Edmund said.

Throck considered for a moment, then said, "That's me."

"Were you engaged by my aunt to find my mother?"

"I was."

"I have found her."

"Did you now?"

"But I haven't found my sister."

Throck frowned. "That's nothing to do with me."

"I need your help," Edmund said.

Throck rubbed the side of his face with a large hand.
"What about that . . . friend of yours. He gone off?"

"Mr. . . . Dupin?"

"If that's his name."

"He won't help me anymore."

"Why's that?"

"He's crazy."

"Is he? Did he find your mother for you?"

"In a way."

"Does he get the reward then?"

"Mr. Throck, I don't know anything about a reward."

"That's as may be." He rubbed the side of his face for a moment. Then he said, "If I help you find your sister will you put in a word for me so that I get it?"

"Mr. Throck I'll do what you tell me to do."

"Your word now. A good word for Mr. Throck."

"I promise."

Throck sat back, gave a grunt of satisfaction, finally pulled a chair near to him. "Well then, what exactly do you want me to do?"

"It's my sister. I want you to make Mr. Dupin find her."

"Thought you said he was crazy."

"But I think he knows where she is."

"You want it out of him then, do you?"

"Yes, sir."

"You sit down here and tell me all about it."

*　　*　　*

When Edmund unlocked the door to the room and stepped inside, Poe was still writing. The boy glanced quickly toward his mother. She lay asleep on the bed.

He came further into the room, then beckoned to Throck — just behind — to follow. When Poe didn't seem to notice their arrival, Edmund approached him. "Mr. Poe," he said softly.

Poe continued to write.

"Mr. Poe," Edmund repeated, raising his voice slightly.

This time Poe lifted his head. Edmund could see from his eyes that he was having a hard time focusing.

"Sometimes," Poe said, "you lose control of your characters. They want to take over. Do what *they* want. It's a question of who is stronger. Writer or character. But it's all right. I'm almost finished with you."

"What?"

"And your sister."

"Mr. Poe, it's me, Edmund. I've brought Mr. Throck."

Poe stared first at the boy, then at the large man who loomed behind him, his bulk magnified in the smallness of the room.

Throck grinned. "Evening to you, Mr. Poe," he said.

*   *   *

"Ah, yes!" Poe said. "They threw me out of the army too. I'd been drinking." He turned to Edmund. "Why did you bring him here? He's no longer part of the story."

"Mr. Poe," Throck said, "this boy here, he says you can tell us where his sister is."

"His sister is here!" Poe snapped, slapping his notebook. He bent to his work. The pen moved over the paper.

Throck looked at Edmund for an explanation.

"He thinks she's in the story he's writing," Edmund said. "Mr. Poe," he went on more urgently, "you can find her. I know you can."

191

"Edmund," Poe cried, flinging down his pen, "*this* is what's important!"

Moving suddenly, Edmund snatched the notebook from under Poe's hand. As though struck, Poe leaped from his chair and tried to grab the book back. Throck was quicker. He stepped in front of Poe and heaved him against the wall.

Poe looked from Edmund to Throck with frightened eyes.

Edmund held the notebook tightly. "Find Sis or I'll destroy it," he said fiercely.

On the bed, Mrs. Rachett stirred, sat up, and looked about in confusion.

Edmund noticed her. "It's all right, Mother," he called. "This is Mr. Throck. He's going to help us find Sis."

Throck turned. "Please to meet you, madam," he said. "And sorry of your misfortunes. Your sister had come to me for help and we was endeavoring to get you for her. And if this man is willing, we'll find your daughter too."

Unexpectedly Poe jumped and grabbed up his carpetbag. "My manuscript," he demanded, his hand outstretched.

Edmund shook his head. "Not until you help us find Sis," he said.

"Be reasonable, sir," Throck suggested. "You want to get on with your work. He wants his sister. I want to get them that got into the bank, for I understand from the lad here that they're connected. Now, if you put your mind to it, it can all be done in one effort."

Poe glared at the man.

"Didn't I tell you," Throck added, "that Throck sees it through."

For a moment Poe's gaze wavered. Then, giving way abruptly, he sank back into the chair.

"Much better," Throck said.

"I must have the notebook," Poe said.

"Help us first," Edmund insisted.

Poe let out a deep breath, closed his eyes, and leaned forward, resting his head in his upturned hands. Then he sat back. He reached for a bottle, but saw that it was empty and put it aside. He looked inquiringly at Throck.

Throck grinned and held up a full bottle, saying, "Help us first."

Poe cleared his throat. "Mrs. Rachett," he said, his voice ragged, "have you any idea where they might have put your daughter?"

Mrs. Rachett shook her head. "I only knew they had put her in the mausoleum," she replied. "When I went there she was gone."

"And you, Mr. Throck," Poe said. "I suppose the boy's told you everything. Do you have any ideas?"

Throck shook his head. "He mentioned some sort of message."

"Message?" Poe echoed.

Edmund said, "The one I found in Mrs. Whitman's house."

Poe looked about, then searched his pockets and retrieved the coded message Edmund had found. He held it out to Throck.

Throck took it and in exchange gave Poe the bottle.

While Poe quickly opened the bottle and drank from it, Throck examined the paper. "I can't read it," he said, handing it back.

Poe glanced mockingly at Edmund before reading the message out loud.

"Meet me at the hotel. I have moved girl and gold. Must leave. Sunrise at six A.M."

Throck grimaced. "The first part may make sense," he said. "But sunrise should come closer to seven o'clock these days."

Poe took out his watch. "It's past two now."

"Five hours," said Throck as if he had observed something profound. Poe nodded. Then to Edmund's dismay, Poe offered Throck the bottle. The night watchman grinned and helped himself to a swallow.

Edmund's mother, on the bed, dropped off to sleep again.

Feeling betrayed, Edmund retreated into a corner and watched as Poe and Throck passed the bottle back and forth. The two men discussed all that had happened. It was as if it were some private matter which had nothing to do with Edmund.

Even as he tried to concentrate on their talk — which grew increasingly slurred — Edmund found himself dozing. He didn't want to. Fought it. All the same, he slept.

20

SUNRISE

AT NEARLY FOUR in the morning Edmund woke with a start and looked about.

His mother was asleep in the bed. Throck, also asleep, was seated on the floor, his head thrown back against a wall, mouth open and snoring. Poe slept too. He was slumped over the table amid several empty bottles, head cradled in his arms, fingers clutching his notebook. The last candle, no more than a stub, was burning low.

Suddenly conscious that much of the night had passed, Edmund ran to the window. Though it was still raining, he decided it must be close to dawn. Alarmed, he turned back to the room. His mother, he realized, would not be able to help. Nor, he saw, would Poe, or Throck.

With growing panic he looked about for something that might help him and noticed the coded message on the table. He snatched it up, but when he confronted the symbols again, his heart sank. Once more he felt engulfed by feelings of fear and insufficiency. He rushed over to Poe and shook him.

"Mr. Poe . . . Mr. Poe . . ." he cried.

Poe continued to sleep.

Edmund, trembling with frustration, gave it up. Taking hold of himself, he placed the message on the table near the candle and racked his brain to remember what Mr. Poe said the symbols meant. Gradually it came back to him:

> Meet me at the hotel. I have moved girl and gold. Must leave. Sunrise at six A.M.

Edmund glanced out the window again, wondering how long it would be before sunrise. For a moment he watched the rain trickle down the window panes. *Where had they put her!*

Once more he gazed around at the sleepers. But this time a thought came to him, something Mr. Throck has said about the hour of sunrise given in the message, that it wasn't *right*. Even as Edmund remembered that, something Mr. Poe had said popped into his head: *"Lies have their own truth."*

Edmund considered the message another time and tried to pry some new meaning out of "Sunrise." Not a lie exactly but some other sense, some other truth. Had Rachett meant, not dawn, but something else? Where had he seen the word *Sunrise* before? *Somewhere* . . . the day before . . . when Peterson had tried to catch him . . .

And suddenly, Edmund remembered.

He hurried over to the table. "Mr. Poe," he whispered.

Poe looked up with only partially open eyes. "What is it?" he managed to say.

"At the docks yesterday," Edmund said, growing more excited, "where Peterson tried to catch me, there was a boat, a sloop. She was called — *Sunrise*."

"*Sunrise?*" Poe repeated, "Is it sunrise already?"

"Mr. Poe," Edmund said, almost begging. "I think *Sunrise* may be a boat."

"Edmund, let me be."

"We have to find my sister!"

"Who?"

"Sis!" Edmund said, shaking him.

"Sis is dead," Poe murmured, clutching his notebook and slumping over it again. "The way it must be."

Edmund let go of him in disgust. Then he went to Throck and shook him hard. "Mr. Throck," he tried. "Wake up." He shook him harder. This time Edmund caught sight of a pistol butt sticking out from his jacket.

Startled, he stepped back. For a moment he just stared at the gun. Then he looked about the room at the two men asleep before him. Edmund shook his head.

Cautiously, he pulled the pistol out of Throck's jacket. It came with surprising ease.

He went back to Poe. "I am going to the docks," he said urgently. "To the *Sunrise*."

". . . too late." Poe mumbled. "Sis is dead."

Anger flamed within Edmund. Taking hold of Poe's notebook he pulled out the pages of new writing, tore them

197

to bits, then flung them on the floor. Poe, oblivious, continued to sleep.

Pistol in hand, Edmund stepped into the hall and shut the door behind him. As the door closed, he heard movement in the room, as if someone had gotten up. He hurried down the steps.

The street was deserted. The light was a lifeless gray. The rain had turned to a swirling web of damp, wet cold. And from somewhere far thunder rumbled.

For a moment Edmund could only stare out onto the bleak scene. Then, after wrapping the pistol into his shirt, he rushed out into the street.

It was about five o'clock when Edmund reached the wharf where he'd seen the sloop *Sunrise*. The place seemed deserted, the quiet broken only by the occasional splash of waves, and the soft moan of wind. He himself was drenched and cold.

But now he was on the wharf Edmund realized that if the boat was still there, he had no idea what he'd do about it.

Then he thought he saw something move. He waited and peered forward. The misty rain made it difficult to see. A light went on. The best Edmund could determine was that at about the middle of the wharf — the very spot where he had seen the two boats the previous afternoon — someone was moving about.

Edmund pulled the pistol from under his shirt and tried to check to see if it was loaded. He thought so, but wasn't sure. Did he need to cock the hammer? Adjust the trigger? He could only hope it hadn't gotten wet. He decided it didn't matter; he was determined to use it somehow if need be.

Closer still, he grew sure that what he saw was a light bobbing up and down on the larger of the two boats. That would be *Sunrise*. His heart beat faster.

The mist began to lift. Now he could see that the boat's forward sail was flapping idly in the wind. And he was able to make out that the figure he'd noticed was crouching on the wharf uncleating a rope. Edmund understood then: the ship was being readied to leave.

He took a few more steps. The person heard, stood up abruptly, and gazed in Edmund's direction.

Edmund froze.

For a few moments the man continued to stare. Then he resumed his work.

Edmund crept on. Now he could see that the man was dressed in rough clothing and a heavy sea jacket — and that his hair was blond white. Mr. Peterson!

His hand on the pistol, Edmund stopped no more than twenty feet from him.

Peterson looked up. "Is that you, Rachett?" he demanded.

Edmund lifted the pistol and pointed it directly at the man, hoping he would see it. "Mr. Peterson?" he called.

"Who is that?"

"I want my sister," Edmund said.

Peterson stood still.

Edmund managed a few more steps, trying with difficulty

to hold the pistol steady. The brightening sky now allowed him to see Peterson quite clearly. And the man saw him.

"Ah, you," he said.

"Where is she?" Edmund demanded.

Peterson offered a most pleasant smile. "Who's that now?"

"My sister."

"Your sister . . ." the man echoed.

"I don't care about the gold," Edmund said, as evenly as he could. "I won't try to stop you. I just want you to let Sis go."

Peterson took a tentative step toward Edmund, who lifted the pistol higher. Peterson stopped. And smiled.

"Is my sister in the boat?"

"We'll wait until Mr. Rachett gets here," the man suggested and turned back to the rope he had been untying.

"I want her!" Edmund called to him.

"It's no crime for a father to have his daughter with him, is it?" Peterson said over his shoulder.

"He's not her father!" Edmund cried. "And she doesn't want to be there. You stole her."

"Believe me, I don't want her. That's Rachett's notion. He thought having her would make our sliding off that much more certain. If it was me, I'd have got rid of her long ago. Like I did the other." He looked about. "Mr. Rachett may be good with plans but he's squeamish about the hard parts. His claim is that you can't play cards without chips. Perhaps he was right. Seems the girl *is* a chip. So, if you put that pistol down," Peterson said with a smile, "it might be possible for you to see her for yourself."

"Is she there then?" Edmund stammered, trying to brace

himself against the gusts of wind which kept pulling and pushing his gun-holding arm.

"I just said, if you put that thing down, we can talk. That's Rachett's point, isn't it? 'I'm a businessman,' he said to me. 'And businessmen bargain. And if one thing doesn't work, try another.' That's his way and he's in charge."

Peterson flung the rope onto the boat where it landed with a thud. A wave lifted the bow and eased it away from the wharf. The wharf timbers creaked. Edmund glanced at the *Sunrise*. She was single-masted, decked-over. Sis, he decided, must be below.

"Well now," Peterson said very casually, "you're welcome to see for yourself." He moved to one of the two remaining ropes that held the boat to the wharf. "Go on," he coaxed. He uncleated it and flung that too on the boat. Only one rope remained.

Edmund, increasingly uncertain and upset, took a step closer.

Peterson backed away and lifted his hands. "I won't touch you," he said.

Trying to keep an eye on Peterson, Edmund inched up to the edge of the wharf and examined the boat. It seemed deserted.

"*Sis!*" he called.

There was no answer, only the slapping of waves on the hull. Edmund glanced quickly over his shoulder at Peterson. The man was merely standing there, looking at him.

"Sis!" Edmund tried again, leaning forward, mindful of his balance. It was then that he was struck from behind.

21

THE CHASE

"EDMUND!"

Edmund opened his eyes. Poe was looming over him. Just behind him was Throck.

"Where are they?" Poe demanded. "Where did they go?"

Still groggy, Edmund struggled to a sitting position. His head hurt badly. "On the boat," he managed to say. "I'm sure they've got Sis."

"Is that them?" Poe asked, pointing toward the river.

Edmund twisted around. Out beyond Fox Point, through the swirl of mist and squally rain, he could make out the *Sunrise* tacking hard against the western marshes.

"I think so," he said, trying unsuccessfully to get to his feet. "Can we get them?" he asked.

"If we're lucky," Throck returned. He stomped down the dock toward the other boat, a sloop-rigged launch named

Peggy. She was a much smaller boat than the *Sunrise*, with considerably less sail.

Poe began to undo the mooring ropes.

For a moment Edmund merely watched, too dizzy, too bewildered to understand what was happening. Then he realized that the men were about to give chase to the *Sunrise* without him. That was enough to propel him to his feet, then hurry to Poe and help him lift the last of the ropes. Throck, meanwhile, had already hoisted the sloop's mainsail, tied it down, and stationed himself at the tiller.

"Come on!" he cried.

Poe freed the last rope, then clambered aboard the boat.

For a brief moment Edmund remained on the wharf, too flustered to move. But as he stood there, the *Peggy*'s sail caught the wind. She began to slide away. "Wait!" he cried and with a leap he jumped, falling into a heap at the bottom of the boat. Then he staggered up to his feet and looked over the side. The *Sunrise* was now moving across the river, out toward the bay.

The *Peggy* followed, spanking the wind-chopped surface of the water with an incessant beat, pitching and yawing, sometimes violently. Edmund struggled toward the helm.

"Can we get them?" he called to Throck a second time.

"We'll try!" Throck boomed out, never taking his eyes from the *Sunrise*. "Wet sails don't help!"

"They have my sister," Edmund said. "I'm sure they do."

"Glad to hear it," answered Throck.

"And the gold."

"Better yet."

"How did you know where I was?"

"He figured it out," said Throck with a nod toward Poe. "In a dream, he said."

Edmund turned. Poe had taken a place before the mainsail. With his wet hair plastered back over his forehead, his greatcoat flowing out behind him, his intense gaze riveted on the *Sunrise* ahead, he stood like a ship's figurehead.

Holding to the thwarts, Edmund went forward to Poe.

"Mr. Poe!" he called above the wind and rain. "Thank you for coming!"

For a moment Poe remained mute. Then he said, "Did you think I would let you make an end to my story?"

"Sir?"

"Why did you destroy my manuscript?"

"You wouldn't help."

"Do you really expect to see your sister alive?"

"She *is* alive. That man Peterson — he's on the boat — he all but said she was."

"Edmund, she has died."

"That's your *story*," Edmund cried. "This is real!"

"Edmund," Poe returned, with just as much vehemence, "you may have destroyed the manuscript but you will not do the same to my story."

Sickened, Edmund turned away, fixing his eyes instead on the *Sunrise*. He could see her tacking back and forth in and out of the mist and rain, edging toward the bay in a southerly direction. Throck, following move for move, held the *Peggy* to their outside, which kept Edmund busy ducking under the shifting boom. Edmund could see for himself that while the *Sunrise* was a bigger boat with more sail, the *Peggy* had greater maneuverability.

"Edmund!" Throck called. "Did you take my pistol?"

Only then did Edmund remember. "They must have taken it from me."

"Then we shall hear of it soon enough," Throck returned.

Edmund watched the *Sunrise*. Now he could see Rachett, at her wheel, turn to look at the *Peggy* as, moment by moment, she gained on them.

Edmund looked over his shoulder toward Poe. The man was simply staring ahead. Edmund was suddenly certain he had some plan in mind.

Edmund made his way back to Throck. "Mr. Throck!" he called

"What's that?"

"You won't do anything Mr. Poe tells you to do, will you?"

"Do you see me here?"

"I do, but . . ."

"And we two made a bargain, didn't we?"

"I know, but . . ."

"Then don't you worry about me."

Edmund gazed at Poe, then at the *Sunrise*. The *Peggy* was still following tack for tack. Lightning and thunder filled the sky. The rain began to intensify.

"As long as we're in the narrows," Throck cried, trying to make himself heard over the weather, "we can work them. But when they get to wider water, into the bay as they're trying to do, they can outrun us sure."

"Can you tell where they're going?"

"The bay. Then the ocean!"

"Can you cut them off?" Edmund returned.

"It's what I'm trying," Throck called. "You might try praying for this muck to lift. If it comes any thicker or stronger I'm likely to lose sight of them. Get yourself up by the jib and be prepared to run her to one side or the other. The faster you can do it, the quicker we'll move."

Edmund started to go.

"And boy! Keep an eye for rocks! They come up at you when you're least aware — especially in shallows. I'll need my eyes for the thieves."

Edmund scrambled to the forward sail, where he saw that Poe was still staring fixedly at the *Sunrise*. The intensity of his look made Edmund's skin prickle.

Throck held to his course. There were times when Edmund lost sight of the *Sunrise* completely. But after moments of breathless suspense, he would see the boat again. And once or twice, when they drew closer to the shore, he made out boulders, their jagged crowns breaking the surface of the water into froth and foam. Each time he cried, "Rocks!"

"See them!" Throck returned.

Sudden gusts of wind brought the rain down in

curtain-like sheets, momentarily obscuring their view. As they tried to batter through the rising waves their pace became lumbering. Lightning and thunder cracked the sky.

Five miles below Providence, the bay widened greatly. The *Sunrise*, reaching the point first, began to come about.

"There!" shouted Throck. "Here's our chance. Watch which way they go!"

Edmund peered over the bow through the storm. He could see for himself that if the *Sunrise* turned successfully, she would have a long run toward the south. The *Peggy* would never be able to match her in speed.

Suddenly, the *Peggy* made a move to starboard. The *Sunrise*, ahead, turned the same direction.

"She's going that way!" Edmund called, pointing west.

In response Throck roared, "Coming about! Throw the jib!"

The sail instantly refilled with wind. The boat heeled; spray and rain blew into Edmund's face and prevented him from seeing. Wiping his wet hair out of his eyes, he searched for the *Sunrise*. He could no longer see her before them. He looked back. Shocked, he saw her there. As the *Sunrise* cut to the west, Throck, instead of following as Edmund expected him to do, cut to the southeast, running as close into the wind as possible. The two boats were going in opposite directions.

Edmund spun about. "They'll get away!" he cried, not understanding what was happening.

"Patience, boy," Throck called. "Patience!"

Edmund stole a look at Poe. The man's face was a tense mask, unreadable.

Edmund turned his eyes toward the *Sunrise* again. The boats continued to sail in opposite directions. Anxiously, he waited for Throck to give orders to pull the jib and resume the chase. But Throck held a steady course.

As Edmund strained to see, he could just barely make out the *Sunrise* coming about sharply and begin to make her move down the bay, bucking wind and waves. It was as if she was following them!

"Mr. Throck!" Edmund cried out in bafflement. "They're chasing us!"

Throck grinned but held steady.

Edmund gripped the ropes tightly, expecting Throck to come about. But to his dismay, Throck continued to hold the *Peggy* on the same southeasterly course, glancing often over his shoulder to judge the two boats' relative positions.

Kneeling on the bow, Edmund could feel his muscles beginning to cramp from tension.

Then he heard Throck cry, "Ready, boy!"

Edmund squeezed the jib lines as tight as he could.

"Coming about!" Throck shouted. Edmund yanked. The jib whipped across the bow. Behind him, the boom swung to the portside with a crack. The *Peggy* came hard about, heeling so deeply that water trickled in over the thwarts. For a moment Edmund thought they were going to capsize, but a second later the boat pulled herself upright. Now the *Peggy* had the wind behind her and was flying *up* the bay

208

with hardly a ripple or sound beneath her bow. To Edmund's astonishment, she was heading straight for the *Sunrise*.

"We've got them!" Throck yelled.

Remembering Poe, Edmund looked around. The man remained wedged firmly against the mast, eyes fixed upon the other boat.

Edmund grew more uneasy.

But now Rachett and Peterson realized what had happened. As the two boats drew rapidly toward each other it was the *Sunrise* that came about with a hard heel which raked her mast dangerously toward the surface of the water as she headed back up the bay toward Providence.

"Trapped them!" Throck exalted.

Even Edmund saw it. "Hurrah!" he cheered. The next moment, however, he heard a bang. At first he thought it was lightning. Then he realized it was Peterson shooting at the *Peggy*. But with both boats moving north, the wind strong from the south, the rain unceasing, and the distance still great, bullets were of no use. Peterson soon gave up.

Once again Rachett shifted his course, heading the *Sunrise* toward the western shore.

"He's heading for shallower water!" Throck cried. "Trying to pull us onto rocks! Watch for them!"

But hardly had the *Sunrise* made that shift than she suddenly came about yet again. Once more the two boats were running head to head.

As Edmund watched, torn between searching for rocks and gazing at the *Sunrise*, he saw Peterson disappear from view. In moments he reappeared. In his arms he was holding someone.

Edmund leaped up. "He's got Sis!" he screamed. She was struggling, but Peterson held her fast.

"Edmund! Keep watching for rocks!" Throck shouted.

But Edmund only had eyes for Sis and the *Sunrise*. The two boats were rushing headlong toward one another, closing rapidly now. The *Peggy* was sailing smoothly while the *Sunrise* seemed to be dancing up and down as if on a prancing horse. Above them lightning cracked and thunder clattered. Rain raked the deck. But so steadily did both boats maintain their courses that Edmund was certain they would collide. He darted a look back at Poe only to realize that the man was now standing just behind him.

Edmund turned again toward the *Sunrise*. Peterson, trying to steady himself, had made his way to the bow and was holding the struggling girl in front of him like a shield even as he held a pistol out in the other hand. Rachett, still at the helm, was yelling at him.

"Mr. Poe! Look out!" Edmund warned, then dropped to the desk.

Poe remained upright, as if daring Peterson to aim at him. Sure enough, Peterson fired. The bullet went astray.

The boats were no more than forty feet apart.

"The girl!" they heard Peterson shout.

Edmund pulled himself up to a kneeling position again and looked. Sis had broken away from Peterson and was scrambling toward the stern of the *Sunrise*. Peterson was in full pursuit. But then, as she approached the helm, Rachett suddenly abandoned the wheel and lunged at her.

With the rudder no longer under control, the *Sunrise* swung wildly about. There was a loud snap and the shriek of tearing wood. Trying to regain control, Rachett flung himself back to the wheel, turning it wildly now this way, now that. As Edmund watched, breathless, Peterson drew close enough to Sis to make a grab for her just as she leaped into the water.

Edmund jumped to his feet. The instant he did, Poe's arms clamped down on him.

"Let me go!" Edmund screamed.

"The story!" Poe cried into his ear. *"The story!"*

Absolutely frantic, Edmund butted and kicked Poe back and, once free, flung himself into the bay. Icy water closed over him, its coldness numbing; he could not move arms or legs. He began to sink, swallowing a mouthful of water. He gagged. The convulsive movement brought back consciousness. He kicked out and swung his arms, pushing himself with swift downward thrusts until his head burst above the water's surface. Once there he thrashed about in search of Sis.

The first thing he saw was the *Sunrise* on her side. She had capsized. And Sis was nowhere to be seen.

"Edmund!" came a cry. "Edmund!"

Edmund turned. Sis was no more than five feet away, working hard to keep afloat. They began to swim toward one another.

Throck, meanwhile, had brought the *Peggy* sharply about in the wind. As if a brake had been applied, the boat stood still, trembling. Now Throck eased her forward, and drew up to them. Hanging over the *Peggy*'s side, he hauled Sis and Edmund into the boat.

The boy looked back over his shoulder just in time to see the *Sunrise* slide beneath the waves.

"They're gone," he heard Throck cry with horror.

As Edmund and Sis huddled together, the *Peggy* sailed beneath the rain toward the dock from which they had started. Edmund, suddenly remembering, looked for Poe.

Poe was staring out over the bay. But then he turned and looked at Edmund. Only then did Edmund realize the man was weeping.

And Edmund knew it was not for Peterson and Rachett.

22

THE BEGINNING OF THE STORY

SIX HOURS LATER Edmund and Poe left Sis and her mother and walked down the steps from the tiny room together. Poe had already announced he was leaving. Now the two of them stood awkwardly on the street.

"Will you and Mrs. Whitman marry now?" Edmund asked.

A pained expression came into Poe's face. "I don't know," he said gravely. "I will fetch the daguerreotype and bring it to her." He shook his head. "But I believe I have too many enemies."

"Why?"

"My art is too strong. I frighten the timid," Poe said, and abruptly began to walk away.

Edmund watched him go. Unable to restrain himself, he called out, "Mr. Poe!"

Poe stopped.

"You never did want to save my sister, did you?" Edmund said. "You only wanted to make sure she'd die."

Poe said nothing.

Edmund felt a swell of disgust. "You're always talking about death," Edmund continued, "but it's living you're frightened of."

Poe turned. His eyes were full of anger. Suddenly he thrust a hand into a pocket and drew out a piece of paper. Edmund recognized it as part of a page from the notebook.

"Edmund, you said I wished your sister to die. I say I wished my story to live.

"I ask you: in what fashion will your sister live longer? In her life? Or, in this, *my* story that would have been? Here is what remains of the story you destroyed." He let the paper flutter to the ground. "Good-bye," he said, turned, and walked away.

Edmund watched him go. When he was sure Poe had truly gone, he went to where the paper lay. After a moment, he picked it up and read what the man had written:

PROLOGUE

At the far back of the top floor of an Ann Street
tenement was a room. It was a small, single-
windowed room, not much warmer than the
outside, for there was only a solitary candle to heat
it. The room contained a table, a chair, and against
one wall, a trunk. Opposite the trunk was a narrow
bed upon which sat a boy. His name was Edgar.

The name Edgar was crossed out. In its place a new name had been inked in:
Edmund.

SOMETHING ABOUT
EDGAR ALLAN POE

POE WAS BORN in Boston in 1809 to actor parents. His father soon after disappeared, and his mother died when Poe was three. Her death was to haunt him all his life. Poe was then taken into the Richmond, Virginia, home of John Allan — hence the name Allan in Poe's name. As a young man Poe acquired a reputation as a gambler and drinker, causing friction between himself and John Allan, whom Poe had come to detest.

Running off to Boston, Poe published some early poems but, unable to find employment, he joined the army. Then, in an attempt at reconciliation with Allan, Poe entered West Point. It was not long before he was expelled from the military academy.

Once again Poe quarreled with Allan and now there was an irrevocable break. Poe went to New York City and then Baltimore where his career as a writer took firm hold; his reputation as a major creator of tales and poems would grow to great heights.

Poe's aunt, a Mrs. Clemm — he sometimes called her Aunty — took him in and became much like a mother to him. It was she who helped to arrange a marriage between Poe and her daughter, Virginia, who was but thirteen. At the time he was twenty-seven and his name for her was "Sis."

It was in 1841 that Poe published "The Murders in the Rue Morgue," considered to be the first detective story. Auguste Dupin, a Frenchman, was his fictional detective. The year 1845 saw publication of his poem, "The Raven," which made Poe America's most famous writer, as well as bringing him international fame.

In 1847 Virginia died. Poe fell into a period of depression and decline, complicated further by his persistent drinking.

In 1848, even as he was falling in love with Mrs. Anne Richmond of Lowell, Massachusetts, Poe went to Providence, Rhode Island, where he courted Mrs. Sarah Helen Whitman. It was in Providence that Poe had a daguerreotype made. This portrait, Mrs. Whitman said, showed Poe "immediately after being snatched back from the ultimate world end of horror."

Over the objections of her mother, Mrs. Powers, and her own friends, Mrs. Whitman and Poe became engaged. But this engagement was ended by Mrs. Whitman herself when Poe broke his pledge not to drink.

A year later, in 1849, Poe died in Baltimore under mysterious circumstances.

AVI's work spans nearly every genre and has received nearly every major prize, including the Newbery Medal for *Crispin: The Cross of Lead* and Newbery Honors for *Nothing But the Truth* and *The True Confessions of Charlotte Doyle*. Avi lives in Denver, Colorado. You can visit him online at www.avi-writer.com.

More Unforgettable Tales from AVI

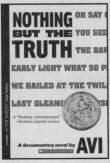

SCHOLASTIC

scholastic.com